P9-CDH-961

GENA/FINN

HANNAH MOSKOWITZ
& KAT HELGESON

CHRONICLE BOOKS
SAN FRANCISCO

Copyright © 2016 by Hannah Moskowitz and Kat Helgeson.
All rights reserved. No part of this book may be reproduced in any form without written
permission from the publisher.

Library of Congress Cataloging-in-Publication Data:
Moskowitz, Hannah, author.

Gena/Finn / by Hannah Moskowitz and Kat Helgeson.

   pages cm

   Summary: "Told through emails, text messages, journal entries, and blog posts, two
fans of a popular TV show become friends online, but soon realize the bond between
them is more than fan fiction in this story of friendship and love through social media in
the digital age"—Provided by publisher.

   ISBN 978-1-4521-3839-8 (hardback)

   [1. Fan fiction—Fiction. 2. Authorship—Fiction. 3. Television programs—Fiction. 4.
Friendship—Fiction. 5. Love—Fiction. 6. Social media—Fiction. 7. Computers—Fiction.]
I. Helgeson, Kat, author. II. Title. III. Title: Gena Finn.

   PZ7.M84947Ge 2016

   [Fic]—dc23

                        2015014236

Manufactured in China.

Illustrations by Avery Wheless.
Design by Ryan Hayes.
Typeset in Brandon Text, Helvetica, and Garamond.
Quotation on page 45: "Everything was beautiful, and nothing hurt." Kurt Vonnegut,
*Slaughterhouse-Five*.

10 9 8 7 6 5 4 3 2

Chronicle Books LLC
680 Second Street
San Francisco, CA 94107

Chronicle Books—we see things differently. Become part
of our community at www.chroniclebooks.com/teen.

FOR THE REAL JAKE AND TYLER

part one

GENA

_EVENIF'S
JOURNAL

I watch a lot of *Up Below* and
write a lot of fanfic and shoot a
lot of heroin. One of those is false.
I do a mean French braid.

# (JAN 5) Are You Kidding Me...?

Okay, what the *shit* was that episode?

I realize that after three seasons I should not be surprised by this bullshit but...ughhhh, after a hiatus LIKE THAT and a cliffhanger LIKE THAT I thought that maybe, just MAYBE, we'd get some kind of emotional closure. Not to mention you can't be knocked out cold for what, TWO DAYS, and then wake up good as new in the next episode. That is not how medicine works, Show. What the hell are they giving Ty and Jake on this damn show and where can I get a hit of it during finals?

In all seriousness, though, it's frustrating. I mean, I'm happy they rescued Sarahbelle, don't get me wrong, but *we knew that was going to happen.* Remember back last season when they actually talked instead of just burning shit down? I'm getting to the point where I like fanfic more than the actual show, and that's pretty disconcerting and I don't really know what to think about that, except right now what I'm pretty sure I'm thinking is WHO THE HELL IS GOING TO WRITE A FIX-IT FIC, AND WHO WILL LINK ME TO IT RIGHT THIS SECOND.

--eve

## 10 Comments

---

*Leave a comment*

**DanniRice**
Uh, you?

**SwingLowMySweet**

I heard Tumbledown was gonna take a crack at it. Honestly I didn't hate it all that much? Idk, I'm like the only person who didn't though so whatever.

**MioMy**

omgggg seiriously why did you make a post without a fic what are you doing to my heart i've been REFRESHING ALL DAY DAMN YOU WOMAN

**Tylergirl93**

please write it please please please. MORE TYLER

> **_EvenIf**
>
> girl I love you but how many times do I need to tell you you are barking up the wrong journal? come to my arms, jakey, etc etc.

> > **Tylergirl93**
> >
> > tylers hotter

**Tumbledown**

No, I've got no time, this is all yours. Please?

> **_EvenIf**
>
> Ha! Plenty of time to read but not write.

> > **Tumbledown**
> >
> > LESS TALKING MORE WRITING

**_EvenIf**

all right all right all right you people, I'll get it done.

TEXT WITH JOHN C.

genaaaa

what

come oooooover

it's a fucking tuesday, put the vodka away.

r u coming out?

where?

guy from smithfield has a car,
mrs. doubtfire is conked out
by the door already

yeah well my dorm's not so
lucky

put on your stripper heels

it's tuesday. my stripper heels
have a weekend only policy

let me borrow your lipstick
though

yeah okay come by. you have
to sneak in the south entrance

what am i an idiot. what r
you gonna do tonight even

writing a paper

sure you are

seriously, what exactly do you
think i'm doing then

john

ew. i'd rather write a paper.

FROM: SHARON MCKLESKY <SMCKLESKY@STONEYHALL.EDU>
TO: GENEVIEVE GOLDMAN <GGOLDMAN@STONEYHALL.EDU>
DATE: TUESDAY, JANUARY 6 4:03 PM
SUBJECT: VIVE LA FRANCE!

Dear Genevieve,

I've looked over your outline for your paper on the French
Revolution (and thank you for turning this in on time! I know how
averse you are to showing early drafts of your work, and I was
hoping having a required outline submission would help you)
and while I think you're chock-full (as we used to say!) of strong
ideas, I'm concerned that the organization of your supports isn't
as strong as it could be. In light of your recent A minus, I want to
make sure you're not allowing yourself to perform at less than one
hundred percent. Colleges can revoke admissions at any time,
you know! Please come see me as soon as you're available--

Best,
Mrs. Sharon McKlesky

FROM: GENEVIEVE GOLDMAN <GGOLDMAN@STONEYHALL.EDU>
TO: SHARON MCKLESKY <SMCKLESKY@STONEYHALL.EDU>
DATE: TUESDAY, JANUARY 6 4:32 PM
SUBJECT: RE: VIVE LA FRANCE!

Hi, Mrs. McKlesky,

Thank you so much for getting back to me so quickly! Tonight
and tomorrow I'm focusing on some work from one of my other
classes, so I won't be able to fully focus on your paper until
Thursday, and since I'm working with a limited time frame I want
to make sure that I'm committing as much time to this paper as
I can! Therefore, I don't think it would be strategic for me to dole
out my thoughts on this paper throughout the week, so at this
point if it's all right I think I'll proceed on my own. I'll make sure to
save your email to remember to make that a priority through my
future drafts. Thank you, and I'll see you in class tomorrow!


Thanks again,
Genevieve Goldman

FROM: GENEVIEVE GOLDMAN <GGOLDMAN@STONEYHALL.COM>
TO: SHARON MCKLESKY <SMCKLESKY@STONEYHALL.COM>
DATE: *NONE. SAVED TO DRAFTS.*
SUBJECT: RE: VIVE LA FRANCE!

Look, McKlesky:

It's Tuesday. It's the day after my fandom Holy Night. Leave me the fuck alone.

--gena

| _EVENIF'S JOURNAL | I watch a lot of *Up Below* and write a lot of fanfic and shoot a lot of heroin. One of those is false. I do a mean French braid. |
| --- | --- |

## JAN 16 The Prettiest Whistles Won't Wrestle the Thistles Undone

**Author:** _EvenIf

**Word Count:** 392

**Summary:** After the Tawley Place fire, Jake needs some time to recover. Tyler makes soup. Some shit gets said out loud. Takes place between 3.11 and 3.12.

**Pairing:** none

**Disclaimer:** I own nothing, I'm a creepy internet person, lock up your babies, etc.

**Author's Note:** I wrote this instead of a French Revolution paper, so I apologize if there are accidental undertones of rebel uprisings or Catholic unrest. Forgive my school, it knows not what it does.

What Tyler really should remember by now is how well bones hold heat.

He never does. It's like every time he wants to believe that he doesn't need to learn anything, every time he acts like this is the last time, like there's no way in hell he's going to be pulling his fucking sidekick Jake burned and twisted from a job gone wrong.

And all the little bastard is saying is, "We got Sarah, we got Sarah," like somehow that's going to change the fact that he's blistered everywhere his shirt isn't stuck to his skin.

But Tyler's making himself be calm because that's what he fucking *does* (because really he does have plans for when this happens because this *always fucking happens*) and he whispers, "That's right, buddy, you did it," while he twists a cap off a tube of ointment and rubs his hands together to warm them up.

"She got out, right? We got her?"

"We got her. And that's the last fucking job we're doing for Evanson, all right? I mean it this time. If he thinks we're gonna do some rescue mission for *Clara*--"

"Ugh, don't mention her, now I'm all nauseous."

"That's because half your skin's sloughed off."

"So dramatic."

"C'mon, up..." He puts his hand on Jake's back, feels his t-shirt starting to peel away like skin, and carefully leans him against his shoulder to rub the warmed ointment over his arm. A sob gets stuck in Jake's throat, and Tyler tucks him in to his neck.

"You did it, kid," Tyler says. "You're a hero."

Jake closes his eyes and breathes out like that's enough, like a little platitude has made his scorched skin and his wrecked throat and the fucked-up world somewhat okay, and sometimes that's enough to get Tyler through the day but right now Jake's stupid optimism is just another symptom of how much the universe has fucked them over. Who the fuck tricked Jake enough to make him think there's something to be *optimistic* about?

It's all he can do not to get up and hit something, and then of course the kid has to mumble a little in his sleep and catch the hem of Tyler's sleeve between brown-black fingernails.

Goddamn it, kid.

This is the kind of shit that will make you believe.

Just for tonight.

## 24 Comments

Leave a comment

**MioMy**
oh my godddddd exactly what I needed. whenever you go into tyler's head like that it's like...gaaahhh i don't have words i am not a writer lolol

> **_Evenlf**
> Oh shut up I love your stuff. Thank you!!

**CalmMyLightsaber**
Lovely. This was great.

> **_Evenlf**
> Hey, I haven't heard from you in ages!! I'm so glad you're still around!

> > **CalmMyLightsaber**
> > I know right shit has been CRAZY. I'll message you sometime?

> > > **_Evenlf**
> > > Yes please!

**Tumbledown**
So worth the wait. (I have a problem and you're incredible.)

> **_Evenlf**
> You're amazing. Next one's on you ;)

**Tylergirl93**
omggggg tyler my baby

> **_Evenlf**
> glad you liked it!

**Thatsmykid**
I just ACHE for them.

**_EvenIf**

right??

**TinyDancer5**

do you write original stuff?

**_EvenIf**

a little, poetry mostly

**TinyDancer5**

good :)

**_EvenIf**

<3

**Neah**

butting in—would you ever post your poetry?

**_EvenIf**

good lord no

**JandT**

do you take constructive criticism?

**_EvenIf**

Take it like it's on sale. What's up?

**JandT**

id really prefer if there were less cursing in your fics. i mean it's not like they talk that way on the show.

**_EvenIf**

thanks! i'll take that under advisement :) and i'll try to remember to put a warning on next time.

**rupologize**

of course they don't talk that way on the show, jackweed. It's network tv.

**_EvenIf**

now now.

FINN

# *finnblueline*

//////////////////////////////////////////////////////////////////////

## January 7th
///////////////////

Okay, guys, calm down.

I get it. I saw it. I'm not thrilled either. I mean, when we last left the guys they were in the middle of a fire and the house was falling down around them and *we didn't know if they were going to make it out oh my god*, except, of course we knew. What show have you guys been watching? They always make it out. That wasn't the point. The point was that scene right after they got out, the one we didn't see, the one where they realized they were gonna be okay and made up after the fight. I wanted to see it too, guys.

And no, it's not credible that Jake was lying unconscious behind a burning dresser and two days later he doesn't have a scratch on him. There's absolutely something missing there and everyone knows it.

But this is our show. This is the show we love, and tearing it apart like hyenas every time the writers do something we don't like is shitty. Do we actually like this show or not?

Can we please talk about the good stuff? The Evanson reveal was kind of mind-blowing, right? Did ANYBODY see that coming? And in other news (and I swear I'm not fourteen but) how cute was Jake's hair this week?

I'm thinking of getting back into drawing, so there might be an art post later this week. I don't know what I want to draw, though. Which is kind of always the problem. Prompts?

Anyway, here are this week's fic recs:
For A Season – evanson_much
Firestorm – Tylergirl93
Hiatus – (it's so ridiculous but I can't stop laughing) – I8gr8

>>>>terry-the-hedgehog reblogged this from finnblueline
>>>>mmmZack reblogged this from finnblueline
>>>>Tylergirl93 reblogged this and added: thanks for the rec!
>>>>DanniRice reblogged this from mmmZack and added: do you
read _EvenIf? Great ep fix here
>>>>slotohes reblogged this from DanniRice
>>>>popstotheweasel reblogged this from Tylergirl93 and added:
ART POST PLEASE!

FROM: STANFORD UNIVERSITY EMPLOYMENT OFFICE
<STAFFINGSERVICES@STANFORDU.EDU>
TO: FINN BARTLETT <FINN.A.BARTLETT@GMAIL.COM>
DATE: WEDNESDAY, JANUARY 7 12:33 PM
SUBJECT: THANK YOU FOR YOUR INTEREST

Dear Ms. Bartlett,

Thank you for your interest in the position of Administrative
Assistant in the Student Affairs Department. After careful review,
we have offered the position to someone whose qualifications
more closely match our needs. We appreciate your interest and
wish you luck.

FROM: DANA WESTCHESTER
<DanaWestchester@DUFFPETERSON.COM>
TO: FINN BARTLETT <FINN.A.BARTLETT@GMAIL.COM>
DATE: FRIDAY, JANUARY 9 8:02 AM
SUBJECT: YOUR RESUME

Stephanie Bartlett,

Thank you for submitting your resume to Duff & Peterson. At this
time we are not hiring entry-level proofreaders, but we will keep
your information on file and let you know if anything becomes
available.

FROM: EVERGREEN TEMP AGENCY
<HIRINGSERVICES@EVERGREEN.COM>
TO: FINN BARTLETT <FINN.A.BARTLETT@GMAIL.COM>
DATE: MONDAY, JANUARY 12 3:41 PM
SUBJECT: IZ11285

To: Ms. Bartlett:

Thank you for your interest in job #IZ11285. After due consideration, we have decided not to pursue your employment with us. Again, thank you for your time.

## TEXT WITH CHARLIE

did you call me?

yeah. should I buy new graphite pencils?

how much?

$10

for pencils?

good pencils

do you have a job yet?

no MOM

well then...

*Jan 8, 3:31 pm*

scratch last. coffee place just called & offered job! bringing home champagne!

FROM: FINN BARTLETT <FINN.A.BARTLETT@GMAIL.COM>
TO: JOAN BARTLETT <JOANBARTLETT4472@GMAIL.COM>;
PAUL BARTLETT <GOHAWKEYESFAN@HOTMAIL.COM>
DATE: *NONE. SAVED TO DRAFTS.*
SUBJECT: CALIFORNIA GIRL!

Hey Parents!

Good news on the job front – I have one! Putting whipped cream and sprinkles on lattes for people more glamorous than I am! Not my field of study – not anybody's field of study – but it pays the bills.

That's a lie. It doesn't pay the bills at all. Even splitting the rent on Charlie's old rat-trap. I would actually sell my computer for a nice apartment, except they don't seem to have those in Northern California (and let's be honest, of course I wouldn't sell my computer).

I went to the beach yesterday, though, just to see what all the fuss was about. God, it's *nothing* like the Lake Michigan beach! It feels stupid to say it, but the ocean is *huge*. (I know, I should have been a poet. My talents are wasted as a barista.) I stood there and felt like I was falling off the edge of the world. But in a good way, if that makes sense.

Tomorrow, Charlie and I

### Text with Mom

got a job yet? ready to give up and come home?

> all moved in with Charlie. start work on Monday.

---

### Private Message to _EvenIf ✕

Um, holy fuck.

I just read your latest fic. Are you in my brain? If so, you can stay. That was just everything I wanted from last week's *Up Below* and didn't get. Thank you, thank you, thank you, etc.

So it's kind of super embarrassing, but I draw occasionally (by which I mean I used to draw four years ago and I'm ridiculously out of practice) and I drew this thing to go along with your fic. It's SUPPOSED to be the part where Jake falls asleep on Tyler at the end, but it looks more like a couple of space aliens.

The self-deprecating thing isn't as charming as I think, is it.

I saw on your journal that you've written a lot of other stuff. Your fans seem a little...hardcore. I guess you must be pretty good. Definitely, if this teeny opus is anything to go by. Psyched to read more, but it's gonna have to wait because I'm in the middle of moving and getting all my shit unpacked.

Okay. This has been sufficiently creepy and weird. I'm attaching the picture. Hope you like it.

Carry on,
finnblueline

GENA/FINN

Hey finnblueline--

holy SHIT this is gorgeous. what the hell, how do you even do that shading? GOD i wish i could draw. this is...god, thank you so much. ridiculously flattering. is it cool if i put a link to this in the author's note of the fic? do you have a journal or something i should link to? your account here looks pretty empty.

your name is seriously familiar though....did you ever write for the Pantheon fandom, or maybe just draw? i wasn't super into Pantheon but i definitely read some stuff.

congrats on the move!

--eve

BUSTED. Yes. I used to draw for Pantheon. I was finnlines over there, added the blue because Jake and Ty are law enforcement (thin blue line) and I love Jake.

But I haven't done anything creative for any fandom since then, and I have no idea if that's supposed to be a brag or a confession. This shit is a drug. Every time I think I'm out, etc etc.

You can absolutely put the pic on your journal if you want. The link is here. Glad you liked it!

Congrats...I dunno, my boyfriend has sketchy taste in apartments. No, seriously, thanks.

jake is like...my love is overwhelming and all-consuming. it's so embarrassing. my friends will be like well how about the new transfer student and i'm just all HOW ABOUT THIS BEAT UP COP ON TV. love him. even if he is an old man.

i'm moving in august and could not be more excited, so i'm jealous even of your sketchiness, probably.

anyway thanks again!! i'll put the link up today.

--eve

---

PRIVATE MESSAGE TO _EvenIf                                    ✕

Oh shit. How old are you?

---

PRIVATE MESSAGE TO FINNBLUELINE                               ✕

eighteen. and actual eighteen, i promise, not internet-eighteen.

--eve

---

PRIVATE MESSAGE TO _EvenIf                                    ✕

Okay. Okay. Sorry, didn't mean to freak out on you. Eighteen's fine. You said Jake was old and I was picturing you as a thirteen year old. Although you write REALLY well for thirteen...

I mean, you write really well for eighteen, too. It's not really an age thing. You write well for a human.

I am FANTASTIC at compliments.

So when you say moving in August, I'm guessing college?

---

PRIVATE MESSAGE TO FINNBLUELINE                               ✕

yep! got into the dreeeeeeam school. mom and dad would be so proud. okay, they probably are, but they're proud over in the taiwanese jungle or whatever the hell so it kind of doesn't count. in all seriousness i'm psyched. i've been at this same school for ten years and i love it, but the problem is that i also really hate it.

and jake's like...what, 28? oooold. although zack's i think 26, right? he always plays older characters. got those old-soul eyes.

so how old are you? i bet you're 28, right?

--eve

---

| PRIVATE MESSAGE TO _EVENIF | ✕ |
|---|---|

Oh thanks very much. No. I'm 22. Just graduated from the very-much-not-dream school, now working the very-much-not-dream job. I miss college and you will love it.

OH MY GOD Zack's eyes. You're probably too young for this, but I've had a crush on him ever since he was a little kid on Man of the House. It's hard to even believe it's still him sometimes, but DAMN that boy grew up good.

---

| PRIVATE MESSAGE TO FINNBLUELINE | ✕ |
|---|---|

ha, yeah, i was pretty little when man of the house was on.

college is really all it's cracked up to be? i'm like afraid to believe it. you wouldn't know from my ridiculous procrastination-project that is my fanfic journal, but i've worked my aassss off these past four years. and kind of the past eight because i go to one of those preparatory boarding schools where if you don't get into an ivy you're ritually sacrificed.

--eve

---

| PRIVATE MESSAGE TO _EVENIF | ✕ |
|---|---|

You're one of those ivy achievers? God. Okay. Well I can only speak for normal person colleges, but yeah, it's great. It's like...remember in season two when Jake was stranded in Costa Rica (GOD survival skills-Jake though...) and Tyler couldn't get there because he was on a no-fly list, so he had to hack into the whatever and erase his record?

Well, college is like that. Whatever you've spent the last eight years thinking you can't do because of who you are and who you've always been, it doesn't apply anymore. You're just this blank nobody-person that you get to invent.

My advice you didn't ask for is do EVERYTHING. Try everything that's offered to you until you find the thing you love. And also, keep writing fic, because my god I just read Mad World and you are blowing my mind.

---

PRIVATE MESSAGE TO FINNBLUELINE ✕

---

aw yeah?? mad world is one of my favorites actually, if i'm allowed to say that about my own stuff...i mean let's be honest the season two finale wrote it for me. where are those I-would-walk-to-the-end-of-the-earth-for-your-damn-self moments in season 3, aaaah i'm dying.

do everything. got it. i'm probably going to be double majoring but it would be nice to find time to get into...something. right now all i get into are tyler girl vs. jake girl battles and lacrosse players' beds. lol overshare.

--eve

---

PRIVATE MESSAGE TO _EVENIF ✕

---

The fuck is lacrosse?

Oh my god do you know Tylergirl93? I link to her stuff on my journal sometimes just to get the exposure. She drives me CRAZY. I think she honestly thinks the show would be better if Jake wasn't on it at all. What is she watching??

With a sort of startling lack of humility, I'm now working on Mad World art. Please tell me to stop if this is annoying.

---

**PRIVATE MESSAGE TO FINNBLUELINE**                                     ✕

oh my god OPPOSITE of annoying. are you going to finish it tonight?? i gotta sign off here in a sec to try to deal with this ridiculous series of emails i'm getting from the aforementioned lacrosse player, but i'll check in first thing tomorrow?

and GOOD LORD DO I KNOW HER. do. i. know her. i have HORROR STORIES, girl. (girl, right? the only finn i know is a guy, but are there even any guys in fandom? what's with that, anyway?)

--eve

---

**PRIVATE MESSAGE TO _EVENIF**                                          ✕

Girl. It's short for Stephanie.

I'll have it finished for you in the morning. Tell me your horror stories, it's only fair.

Good luck with Monsieur LaCrosse!

---

**PRIVATE MESSAGE TO FINNBLUELINE**                                     ✕

ugh, thank you, i need it.

night!!

---eve

GENA

FROM: GENEVIEVE GOLDMAN <GGOLDMAN@STONEYHALL.EDU>
TO: JOHN CLIFFORD <JCLIFFORD@STONEYHALL.EDU>
DATE: SATURDAY, JANUARY 24 12:12 AM
SUBJECT: BACK OFF

> okay, seriously, you're emailing me now? are we having a "how many methods of harassment is enough" contest?

FROM: JOHN CLIFFORD <JCLIFFORD@STONEYHALL.EDU>
TO: GENEVIEVE GOLDMAN <GGOLDMAN@STONEYHALL.EDU>
DATE: SATURDAY, JANUARY 24 12:52 AM
SUBJECT: RE: BACK OFF

> yeah, if you hate it so much why do you answer

FROM: GENEVIEVE GOLDMAN <GGOLDMAN@STONEYHALL.EDU>
TO: JOHN CLIFFORD <JCLIFFORD@STONEYHALL.EDU>
DATE: SATURDAY, JANUARY 24 12:55 AM
SUBJECT: RE: BACK OFF

> i got sick of my phone yelling like something important is going on. stop emailing me.

FROM: JOHN CLIFFORD <JCLIFFORD@STONEYHALL.EDU>
TO: GENEVIEVE GOLDMAN <GGOLDMAN@STONEYHALL.EDU>
DATE: SATURDAY, JANUARY 24 12:56 AM
SUBJECT: KISS & MAKE UP?

> come over.

FROM: GENEVIEVE GOLDMAN <GGOLDMAN@STONEYHALL.EDU>
TO: JOHN CLIFFORD <JCLIFFORD@STONEYHALL.EDU>
DATE: SATURDAY, JANUARY 24 12:59 AM
SUBJECT: RE: KISS & MAKE UP?

> cut it out.

FROM: JOHN CLIFFORD <JCLIFFORD@STONEYHALL.EDU>
TO: GENEVIEVE GOLDMAN <GGOLDMAN@STONEYHALL.EDU>
DATE: SATURDAY, JANUARY 24 1:05 AM
SUBJECT: RE: KISS & MAKE UP?

i'm serious, okay? to talk. Just to talk. If you try to take your clothes off I'll shield my eyes.

FROM: GENEVIEVE GOLDMAN <GGOLDMAN@STONEYHALL.EDU>
TO: JOHN CLIFFORD <JCLIFFORD@STONEYHALL.EDU>
DATE: SATURDAY, JANUARY 24 1:06 AM
SUBJECT: RE: KISS & MAKE UP?

you're drunk.

FROM: JOHN CLIFFORD <JCLIFFORD@STONEYHALL.EDU>
TO: GENEVIEVE GOLDMAN <GGOLDMAN@STONEYHALL.EDU>
DATE: SATURDAY, JANUARY 24 1:08 AM
SUBJECT: RE: KISS & MAKE UP?

No, Gena, I'm not.

FROM: GENEVIEVE GOLDMAN <GGOLDMAN@STONEYHALL.EDU>
TO: JOHN CLIFFORD <JCLIFFORD@STONEYHALL.EDU>
DATE: SATURDAY, JANUARY 24 1:14 AM
SUBJECT: OOOOOH

capital letters. serious business.

FROM: JOHN CLIFFORD <JCLIFFORD@STONEYHALL.EDU>
TO: GENEVIEVE GOLDMAN <GGOLDMAN@STONEYHALL.EDU>
DATE: SATURDAY, JANUARY 24 1:16 AM
SUBJECT: RE: OOOOOH

Come over and we'll talk.

FROM: GENEVIEVE GOLDMAN <GGOLDMAN@STONEYHALL.EDU>
TO: JOHN CLIFFORD <JCLIFFORD@STONEYHALL.EDU>
DATE: SATURDAY, JANUARY 24 1:19 AM
SUBJECT: RE: OOOOOH

that's what you always say, and then it's 5 in the morning and i'm sneaking back into my dorm and my shirt's on inside out and my mouth tastes like shame and secondhand vodka

FROM: JOHN CLIFFORD <JCLIFFORD@STONEYHALL.EDU>
TO: GENEVIEVE GOLDMAN <GGOLDMAN@STONEYHALL.EDU>
DATE: SATURDAY, JANUARY 24 1:23 AM
SUBJECT: RE: OOOOOH

Sounds like your poetry.

FROM: GENEVIEVE GOLDMAN <GGOLDMAN@STONEYHALL.EDU>
TO: JOHN CLIFFORD <JCLIFFORD@STONEYHALL.EDU>
DATE: SATURDAY, JANUARY 24 1:24 AM
SUBJECT: RE: OOOOOH

fuck off, it does not.

FROM: JOHN CLIFFORD <JCLIFFORD@STONEYHALL.EDU>
TO: GENEVIEVE GOLDMAN <GGOLDMAN@STONEYHALL.EDU>
DATE: SATURDAY, JANUARY 24 1:25 AM
SUBJECT: OH CALM DOWN

Meant that as a compliment, relax. I still have the poem you wrote
me.

FROM: GENEVIEVE GOLDMAN <GGOLDMAN@STONEYHALL.EDU>
TO: JOHN CLIFFORD <JCLIFFORD@STONEYHALL.EDU>
DATE: SATURDAY, JANUARY 24 1:26 AM
SUBJECT: RE: OH CALM DOWN

I didn't write it for you. I wrote it and gave it to you.

FROM: JOHN CLIFFORD <JCLIFFORD@STONEYHALL.EDU>
TO: GENEVIEVE GOLDMAN <GGOLDMAN@STONEYHALL.EDU>
DATE: SATURDAY, JANUARY 24 1:27 AM
SUBJECT: RE: OH CALM DOWN

Capital letters. Serious business.

FROM: GENEVIEVE GOLDMAN <GGOLDMAN@STONEYHALL.EDU>
TO: JOHN CLIFFORD <JCLIFFORD@STONEYHALL.EDU>
DATE: SATURDAY, JANUARY 24 1:28 AM
SUBJECT: RE: OH CALM DOWN

What the fuck do you want, john?

I want you to write me another poem.

john john
please go away
do not stay
another day

no capitals.

cummings.

what?

does not mean what you want it to mean.

FROM: JOHN CLIFFORD <JCLIFFORD@STONEYHALL.EDU>
TO: GENEVIEVE GOLDMAN <GGOLDMAN@STONEYHALL.EDU>
DATE: SATURDAY, JANUARY 24 2:14 AM
SUBJECT: SERIOUSLY GEN

just come over.

talk to me. i've been thinking this over, okay? i made a huge
fucking mistake.

FROM: GENEVIEVE GOLDMAN <GGOLDMAN@STONEYHALL.EDU>
TO: JOHN CLIFFORD <JCLIFFORD@STONEYHALL.EDU>
DATE: SATURDAY, JANUARY 24 2:20 AM
SUBJECT: RE: SERIOUSLY GEN

yeah, you've mentioned.

FROM: JOHN CLIFFORD <JCLIFFORD@STONEYHALL.EDU>
TO: GENEVIEVE GOLDMAN <GGOLDMAN@STONEYHALL.EDU>
DATE: SATURDAY, JANUARY 24 2:28 AM
SUBJECT: RE: SERIOUSLY GEN

I still love you.

FROM: GENEVIEVE GOLDMAN <GGOLDMAN@STONEYHALL.EDU>
TO: JOHN CLIFFORD <JCLIFFORD@STONEYHALL.EDU>
DATE: SATURDAY, JANUARY 24 2:31 AM
SUBJECT: RE: SERIOUSLY GEN

okay

FROM: JOHN CLIFFORD <JCLIFFORD@STONEYHALL.EDU>
TO: GENEVIEVE GOLDMAN <GGOLDMAN@STONEYHALL.EDU>
DATE: SATURDAY, JANUARY 24 2:31 AM
SUBJECT: RE: SERIOUSLY GEN

do you still love me?

FROM: GENEVIEVE GOLDMAN <GGOLDMAN@STONEYHALL.EDU>
TO: JOHN CLIFFORD <JCLIFFORD@STONEYHALL.EDU>
DATE: SATURDAY, JANUARY 24 2:42 AM
SUBJECT: RE: SERIOUSLY GEN

i guess

FROM: JOHN CLIFFORD <JCLIFFORD@STONEYHALL.EDU>
TO: GENEVIEVE GOLDMAN <GGOLDMAN@STONEYHALL.EDU>
DATE: SATURDAY, JANUARY 24 2:45 AM
SUBJECT: RE: SERIOUSLY GEN

are you still mad?

FROM: GENEVIEVE GOLDMAN <GGOLDMAN@STONEYHALL.EDU>
TO: JOHN CLIFFORD <JCLIFFORD@STONEYHALL.EDU>
DATE: SATURDAY, JANUARY 24 2:47 AM
SUBJECT: RE: SERIOUSLY GEN

not really

FROM: JOHN CLIFFORD <JCLIFFORD@STONEYHALL.EDU>
TO: GENEVIEVE GOLDMAN <GGOLDMAN@STONEYHALL.EDU>
DATE: SATURDAY, JANUARY 24 2:50 AM
SUBJECT: RE: SERIOUSLY GEN

so...can we get back together?

FROM: GENEVIEVE GOLDMAN <GGOLDMAN@STONEYHALL.EDU>
TO: JOHN CLIFFORD <JCLIFFORD@STONEYHALL.EDU>
DATE: SATURDAY, JANUARY 24 3:01 AM
SUBJECT: RE: SERIOUSLY GEN

this is a bullshit conversation.

FROM: JOHN CLIFFORD <JCLIFFORD@STONEYHALL.EDU>
TO: GENEVIEVE GOLDMAN <GGOLDMAN@STONEYHALL.EDU>
DATE: SATURDAY, JANUARY 24 3:03 AM
SUBJECT: RE: SERIOUSLY GEN

so come over.

nah.

GENA/FINN

hey. i have kind of an obnoxious question.

Shoot

i had a ridiculously shitty night, can you draw me a picture of like...
jake on a llama or something.

On a llama??

I mean, I guess. The heart wants what it wants, right?

Also, here's the *Mad World* picture. It's supposed to be the part
where Jake asks if he's crazy.

What happened? Was it LaCrosse?

ohhhhh my god it's gorgeous. llama picture is officially optional because my heart has been TOO SHATTERED BY THIS TO APPRECIATE IT ANYWAY. gaaah crazy jake, come to my arms. i don't know how i ever make myself write about anything else. Seeing jake like that was just...god. some of the best acting zack's ever done, if you ask me. he just NAILED it. and i'm just like MORE MORE MORE please. if i were in charge of the show it would be such a problem for anyone who wanted, like, plot.

in fact it was. kind of. it's complicated. he sent me this long string of emails trying to get me to come over and then he called me crying about how he's still in love with me and like...do you ever get the feeling that there's something just so fucking CHILDISH about being in love? i feel too old for this shit, or maybe just too old for this high school version of it. i'm just ready to get up and move on, but apparently, as i was told this morning (while gathering my clothes off his floor, hooray willpower), that makes me a heartless bitch!

but...i don't know. i honestly don't think i care that he loves me or whether or not i like him, so maybe i am a heartless bitch.

sorry for shitting my life all over your morning. you at work? am i interrupting? don't get fired for drawing llama pictures.

I'm a barista, and I'm off today. I wouldn't be drawing at work, I'd be kowtowing and pouring drinks like a wage slave.

Do I ever get the feeling there's something childish about being in love...

I've been with my boyfriend (his name is Charlie and he's a lovely person) for three years now, and "in love" doesn't feel like an event anymore. I honestly don't remember what it felt like when this was new. I adore Charlie, and I'm pretty sure he's the proverbial One (I think, maybe, probably) but being in a relationship at this stage is like being enrolled in something. I've signed up for Charlie. And it's not that I regret it or anything, but he's not likely to be moved to tears by anything having to do with me.

And neither am I.

I don't know if that's mature or just sad.

---

PRIVATE MESSAGE TO FINNBLUELINE     ✕

i don't think it's sad. maybe you guys still have that fairy tale moment yet to come. you walk down the stairs in the ball gown, he turns around and his face lights up...i'm not even totally kidding about this is the ridiculous part. i'm like the childish pot calling the childish kettle black here. i don't know. i don't believe in a cute boy in the next dorm but i believe in going to a ball and getting swept off my feet. maybe i've seen dirty dancing too many times. the hazards of being a rich jewish girl.

wish i were off today. i have a french oral report. i cannot wait to never take french again. what did you major in? sorry if i'm being weird and interrogatory. i can shut up.

--eve

---

PRIVATE MESSAGE TO _EVENIF     ✕

You're fine.

I majored in art history. Call me if you need an analysis of a mosaic; otherwise I'm not good for much and neither is my bank account. I'd do it again, though. The thing about a useless degree is that you get to stop worrying about competition and relative success (it so doesn't matter at all whether my classmates understand Cimabue better than I do) and just learn stuff you're interested in.

What's your double major in? No, let me guess—law and medicine. You'll be the world's foremost forensic lawyer. Or doctor immune to lawsuits.

...Okay, here's the llama picture. I put Tyler and Evanson in there too just for laughs. DO NOT POST THIS ANYWHERE. For your eyes only.

PRIVATE MESSAGE TO FINNBLUELINE　　　　　　　　　✕

oh my god evanson riding bitch. HE SO WOULD. thank you thank you thank you this is amazing.

close, kinda--psych and early childhood development. i was kind of a weird little kid and i had some really good doctors who helped me. it was a pretty fucked up time. my parents tried to act like it was just stress or whatever but then i started having hallucinations so off to the doctors i went. i'm fine now. meds every day and all that, and even my shrink says i probably don't need them anymore, because lots of people who have hallucinations when they're kids grow up totally normal, etc., but what can i say, better safe than sorry, right? and it's a convenient reason not to drink when i'm out with my friends. if i do want to drink it's going to be in college, not at some imitation-kegger with boarding-school kids hiding in a townie's basement after hours.

did you meet charlie in college or is he a creepy internet weirdo like us?

---

PRIVATE MESSAGE TO _EvenIf                                    ✕

...That was heavy. I mean, it's fine, but is it weird that this is getting so personal? I don't know. I don't make internet friends. I hope I'm not offending you too much right now, because I like that you told me that stuff. I guess I'm just surprised that you did, or maybe surprised that I like it...now who's being too forthright?

I met Charlie during college, though not actually in college. He was the local bartender. I could not be more of a cliché if I tried. Anyway, he moved out here around the middle of last year, and after graduation I decided to come too. That might've had more to do with California than with Charlie, though. I'm not sure I'd have been so eager to fly the coop if he was moving to Nebraska. Then again, I really hated the coop.

---

PRIVATE MESSAGE TO finnblueline                              ✕

ooh, i've never been to california. quid pro quo i'm in connecticut, so for what it's worth you'd have a much easier time finding me and murdering me.

you've never made internet friends, though? i've got like ten people who know that shit about me, and most of them aren't ones i know in real life. i don't know, i'm not exactly close to anyone, but it feels pretty safe to open up to people when it's just words. and i'm not usually afraid of alienating people because i'm an independent woman, etc. i'm good.

plus i'm not embarrassed really. i mean...how do you stay embarrassed after this long? and like, the girl down my hall isn't ashamed of taking her thyroid replacement thing with breakfast, why should i be ashamed of my anti-psychotics and vaguely diagnosed schizoaffective tendencies?

| PRIVATE MESSAGE TO _EVENIF | ✕ |
|---|---|

Huh. Point Eve.

The thing is that the Pantheon fandom is a lot of teenagers. And I'm not going to talk to teenagers (under 18, kid) online, for obvious reasons. I blog about *Up Below*, but if you've read my blog you've probably noticed I have a lot of unpopular opinions, so people don't reach out a lot. And Charlie doesn't know I'm involved in fandom at all, which limits what I can do.

But obviously your shit's safe with me. Who am I gonna tell?

I like you, Eve. I think I won't murder you.

| PRIVATE MESSAGE TO FINNBLUELINE | ✕ |
|---|---|

wait, charlie doesn't know?? how the hell does that work? even monsieur lacrosse knows (let's call him by the code name "john" from here on out--conveniently his real name, look at that) and we were a couple for like four months a year ago. it's an easy excuse when i want to stay in. LEAVE ME ALONE I'M WATCHING MY STORIES. STAY OFF MY LAWN. etc.

i like you too.

| PRIVATE MESSAGE TO _EVENIF | ✕ |
|---|---|

Oh, it's a lot of awkwardness and half-truths. He knows I'm a fan, obviously. It's hard to hide it on Monday nights when I'm practically making out with the TV. I think he thinks I think Jake is hot. I mean, I DO think that, but it's not...the point, you know?

He doesn't know I blog, and he definitely doesn't know I draw (there are laws about looking at my sketchpad, he probably thinks I'm doing still lifes or something). He knows I spend way too much time on my computer, but who doesn't do that?

...Whoa. It just occurred to me that maybe Charlie also has a secret life on his computer.

---

**PRIVATE MESSAGE TO FINNBLUELINE** ✕

---

to be honest i kind of judge people who don't have secret lives on their computer. no offense to your boyfriend, of course, but i always wonder if they might be kind of...boring. even my friend Alanah has an obsessive shoe blog no one knows about. people need to have different identities, i think. and the bigger deal you make about being open about, like, mental illness or fangirling, the easier it is to get everyone to leave you alone about stuff that's really private. i have no need for anyone to know every part of me. pieces for everyone where they fit works out easiest for everyone.

FINN

hey working girl

whatcha doin?

making bacon

playing world of warcraft

thinking about you

naked?

naked baconing is a horrible idea

ha, no, thinking about me naked

in the purple dress

from jason's wedding? not sexy

beautiful

*Feb 7, 2:44 pm*

you busy?

yeah sorry, swarm of people. gone now

boss gonna get mad at you for texting?

he's not here

cool.

*Feb 7, 2:51 pm*

do you have a secret double life?

yes I'm batman

seriously. do you have secrets?

what kind of secrets?

any. what do you do all day when I'm not there?

bacon. WOW. think about you.

you need a hobby

what do you do at night while I'm at the bar?

I'm a spy

seriously

### Text with Dad

plans for spring break?

I'm out of school dad, no spring break

### Text with Charlie

I really want to know. what do you do?

### Text with Dad

take time off? we'd like to see you!

can't. maybe a weekend?

### Text with Charlie

wait, am I your target? are you spying on me?

yes

that's why I want to know what you do all day

foiled again

*Feb 7, 3:11 pm*

do you have, like, warcraft friends?

sure, my guild

do they know about me?

what about you?

like, that I exist

they're not real people

they are

internet people

*Feb 7, 3:27 pm*

you pissed?

lol no course not

gotta clean the shake machine, I'll see you at home.

love you

## Text with Dad

how the hell do I get email on this phone?

haha call me tonight.

GENA

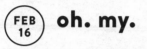

## FEB 16 — oh. my.

I don't even...I don't even have any idea what to say.

THANK YOU, UP BELOW GODS, THANK YOU THANK YOU THANK YOU. Except also hey what am I going to do with my life because I'm pretty sure after that episode I will NEVER NEED FANFIC AGAIN. Is this a secret plot to get me to leave my dorm? IT WON'T WORK, SHOW GODS. Because I need to stay here and JOURNAL ALL MY FEELINGS.

God. Okay. Where to start. The way Tyler just *forgave* Jake for everything? Jake's been carrying around all this guilt for so long and Tyler just took all of the weight off him and like...evaporated it. Good lord I'm eloquent today. But seriously, I know we've all been hoping that somehow Jake's guilt for what happened in the freaking PILOT would be dealt with somehow, but this is like...I swear I've read this actual situation in a fic somewhere. Do you guys know what I'm talking about? Who wrote it agghhh help me out. Purple journal. This is killing me now.

Anyway I loved that fic when I read it and now I can LOVE IT IN REAL LIFE.

Or whatever *Up Below* is. I'm going with real life.

I think what really shanked me in the heart was Jake's REACTION to being forgiven, actually. I don't think we really saw until that moment just HOW MUCH he not only needed it but also never expected that would happen. He's seen Tyler go through hell for him again and again but he never thought that he'd be forgiven for this. He thought this was something that even Tyler couldn't fix. And like...HE FIXED IT. God I love them. I love them so much. And I'm so glad that we know now Tyler isn't angry at him anymore. Maybe fandom will give it a rest now? That'd be nice.

In conclusion, to quote a writer who is in all honestly less talented than the lovely man and lovely lady who wrote last night's ep: EVERYTHING IS BEAUTIFUL AND NOTHING HURTS.

--eve

## 9 Comments

Leave a comment

**YoureaBlur**
OH MY GOD I KNOW RIGHT

> **_EvenIf**
> UNABLE TO DEAL

**StrawberryBlossom19**
It's a _beautifuleyedea_ fic you're thinking of I think. Link here.

> **_EvenIf**
> YES, that's it, thank you. Gorgeous.

>> **StrawberryBlossom19**
>> No problem! She's incredible.

**JakeyBoBakey**
JAKE THOUGH. JUST.

> **_EvenIf**
> I DON'T KNOW HOW I WROTE WORDS WHEN THERE ARE NO WORDS

**Tylergirl93**
messaging you.

>> **_EvenIf**
>> Okay.

FROM: ESME PREVOT <EPREVOT@STONEYHALL.EDU>
TO: GENEVIEVE GOLDMAN <GGOLDMAN@STONEYHALL.EDU>
DATE: FRIDAY, FEBRUARY 20 3:50 PM
SUBJECT: TRES BIEN!

Dear Genevieve,

Lovely work on your oral presentation. A.

Best,
Ms. Esme Prevot

FROM: GENEVIEVE GOLDMAN <GGOLDMAN@STONEYHALL.EDU>
TO: ESME PREVOT <EPREVOT@STONEYHALL.EDU>
DATE: FRIDAY, FEBRUARY 20 4:25 PM
SUBJECT: RE: TRES BIEN!

Merci! Passez un bon week-end!
Best,
Genevieve Goldman

## TEXT WITH MICHELLE Q.

hey whore

hey...woman of the night

diner at 6? Alanah and niya
and me

can't, dr's appointment.
granola bar dinner for me

crazy dr?

that's the one

good luck with that

no need

Hey Genevieve--

Haven't touched base in a while, heard of something that
sounds great for you, wondering if you've decided to make your
big comeback? Paper towel commercial, looking for a sullen
teenager, under five-two, dark straight hair...sounding familiar?
Gimme a call and we'll set up an audition.

Thanks,
Kyle Marksborough
M & D Talent Agency

FROM: Gena Goldman <genazeporah@gmail.com>
TO: Kyle Marksborough <KGMarks@MDTalent.com>
DATE: Friday, February 20 4:15 PM
SUBJECT: RE: Audition

Yo Kyle--

Nope!

Talk later,
Genevieve

*Patient Notes—February 23rd*

## Dr. Rachaela Bachman, PhD

*Patient is, as usual, in good spirits, well put-together,
reporting strong grades. Denies having any recent
psychiatric symptoms, admits to being under quite a bit
of school-related stress, responds quickly and fluently to*

*questions. I'm still concerned that she might be putting too much focus into college as the solution to any anxiety she's feeling. Concerned about her enthusiasm for starting over and worried she's planning to cut too many ties.*

*Patient, as usual, shows reluctance to begin stepping down medication dosages.*

*Follow-up scheduled for March 20th.*

FROM: GENEVIEVE GOLDMAN <GGOLDMAN@STONEYHALL.EDU>
TO: NAOMI HOOLE-GOLDMAN
<NAOMI.HOOLE.GOLDMAN@GMAIL.COM>
DATE: MONDAY, FEBRUARY 23 9:12 PM
SUBJECT: (NO SUBJECT)

Hey Mom,

How's the wilderness? Tripping on any wild berries yet?

All's fine here. A on my French oral report; Prevot finally decided to turn the grades in. Had a doctor's appointment this afternoon, that went fine. Went to dinner with Alanah and the girls and gossiped about boys and the like. There's a boy in my Chem class I think is cute. So stuff's good.

Write back when you have the chance?

Love,
Gena

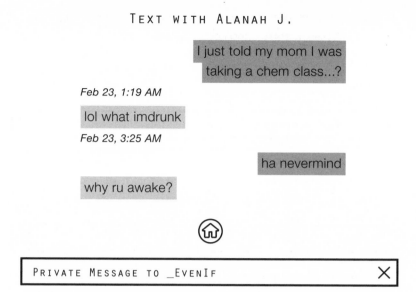

I just told my mom I was taking a chem class...?

*Feb 23, 1:19 AM*

lol what imdrunk

*Feb 23, 3:25 AM*

ha nevermind

why ru awake?

---

PRIVATE MESSAGE TO _EVENIF ✕

okay so i'm sorry but i don't get it. are we seriously just expected to forgive jake now just because he cried his way into making tyler say it? jake STABBED HIM IN THE BACK, you cant actually be one of the crazy people saying thats okay. write a fix-it fic? please? for me?

--mallory

---

PRIVATE MESSAGE TO TYLERGIRL93 ✕

ugh, seriously? He didn't stab him in the back. I'm like blue in the fingers from defending him on this one, I can't believe it's still necessary. In his heart he was on Tyler's side the whole time, but he HAD to trust Evanson's people over Ty's or both him AND tyler would have been totally fucked, and if tyler had known he was doing it to defend him he would have stopped him and tried to protect him. jake had to act like he'd actually decided to go against him. they needed an in and jake was the one willing to be the bad guy for a while for the sake of saving their asses. thank GOD tyler isn't still pissed at him, and I can't believe fandom still is, tbh. No fix-it.

--eve

---

PRIVATE MESSAGE TO _EvenIf                                          ✕

---

is it so much to ask that you step out of your jakegirl comfort zone just ONCE? we're hurting over this one. there's way more of us than you, your audience could be way bigger.

---

PRIVATE MESSAGE TO TYLERGIRL93                                      ✕

---

cry me a fucking river.

---

PRIVATE MESSAGE TO FINNBLUELINE                                     ✕

---

TALK TO ME ABOUT THAT EPISODE because i am dying of feelings and also of fucking TYLERGIRL NEGATIVITY. remind me that i don't hate fandom, please.

how's things? you're not mad at me for implying charlie's boring, are you? i seriously didn't mean to. i read over my message later and hated myself.

--eve

GENA/FINN

I totally hate fandom sometimes.

Do you follow popstotheweasel at all? She's this tylergirl whose journal I read, mostly because she reads mine. Well, the episode wasn't even over and she already had a post up about how ABUSIVE Jake is to Tyler and how inconsiderate of his feelings and how he's just holding Tyler back in everything they do.

I mean, this episode was yesterday. I haven't even organized my thoughts yet. I don't know how people summon up that much hatred that fast for a thing they supposedly love.

Please don't beat yourself up about the Charlie thing. He is boring :)

boring can be nice! (so no secret internet life, then?)

i want to say some kind of "can't we all just get along" thing but the truth is i say shit about tyler that's as bad as what they're saying about jake sometimes but like...it's JAKE, you know? he's this fucking brave kid who's always had tyler there to clean up his messes but NEVER let himself get complacent, and he's got all this courage to strike out on his own and DEFEND tyler and just be the big damn hero tyler always wanted him to never have to be and just...seriously, Show, what? this is almost as bad as the girls who just watch hoping they'll take their shirts off. don't get me started.

Secret internet life, such as it is, apparently consists of playing Warcraft and not exchanging names with a bunch of gamers. He says the only thing they talk about is stuff like PvP stats and goblin keep sieges.

I guess it makes sense. That stuff doesn't integrate with his regular life the way fandom does, I think. I mean, a lot of the guys he plays with are people he knows in real life, but they also hang out and do other stuff and there are whole days where the game doesn't even come up. Whereas I've kind of always got Jake in the back of my mind.

Is that pathetic? It's just that Jake gives me all these FEELINGS, you know? Like, the other day I was at work and incredibly bored and I started thinking about that time in season one when Jake got caught in that rope in the water and Tyler had to jump in after him even though he can't swim, and Jake was so vulnerable and sweet wrapped up in Tyler's stupid flannel jacket...were tylergirls not watching that episode?

| PRIVATE MESSAGE TO FINNBLUELINE | X |
| --- | --- |

they probably blame jake for getting tyler all cold and wet, poor baby. (although i kind of like when my favorite characters are miserable? i promise i don't want ACTUAL PEOPLE to be miserable. but then tyler takes care of him and it's so nice...)

goddddd that episode, i don't know if i love you or hate you for reminding me.

i can't really imagine my life without fandom at this point, and maybe i should mention that to my shrink or something but like... it doesn't feel like a problem. it's a thing that i do. my whole life is little things that i do. sorry, aforementioned shrink made me all melancholy and introspective. it's okay.

tell me about you, how's life?

I love when Tyler gets all caretakery. It's something about the purity of that bond, you know? The way he'd do anything for Jake, literally. As complicated as their lives are, that's this really simple thing they can fall back on.

I don't know why you'd need to mention that to your shrink, but... I've never been to one, so I don't know whereof I speak, here. This isn't me saying I'm too sane for therapy or anything (ha!), it's just not something I've ever done. What's it like? Do you hate it? I feel like I would hate it.

Wow, shut up, Finn. You really don't have to answer ANY of that, I'm sorry.

Life's the same. Charlie's at work until 4 am and I'm staying up to wait for him because otherwise we never see each other. But I really can't complain, because he's paying 70% of the rent on this place. Even though the fact that our rent is as high as it is, is completely his fault, because he ABSOLUTELY HAD to have a two-bedroom in case we get guests or a dog we decide we don't want to see or something.

no no it's cool. what i do isn't exactly therapy--i did that for a while, but that's more of a weekly thing where you go and talk about your feelings and shit. not knocking that, but right now i don't really have feelings worth discussing. what i do is, i go in once a month, she asks me to rate my mood one to ten and am i seeing things or whatever, i say no, we smile at each other, she writes the prescription. it's ten minutes tops.

so finn is such a badass nickname. do you use it in real life? eve's not my real name. technically it could be a nickname of my full name, i guess, but it's not one i use. i didn't even do that on purpose, _evenif just kind of morphed into that when people were talking to me.

I do, yeah. There were three Stephanies in my fifth grade class and I was sick of being Steph B. My mom haaaates it. She says it's a boy's name and she won't use it, but I've had it so long that anything else just doesn't sound like me.

So...what's your name, then? Obviously, you don't have to tell me if you don't want.

(Can we just establish a you-don't-have-to-tell-me policy so I don't have to say it every time?)

PRIVATE MESSAGE TO FINNBLUELINE          ✕

i don't know if i'm private really, i'm just not used to having to tell people things, or like small talk or whatever. my class has 41 kids in it and most of us have been here since the beginning of middle school. we're so bad at talking to anyone who doesn't already know everything about us, it's ridiculous. you should hear us trying to make phone calls.

genevieve. or gena, pronounced like jenna. i use both about the same.

PRIVATE MESSAGE TO _EVENIF          ✕

Fancy. I'm gonna call you Eve.

✉

0055

FINN

/////////////////////////////////////////////////////////////////////////////////////////

February 19th
/////////////////////////

So let's talk about what just happened here.

Shouldn't this have been the moment that united everyone in this fandom? I mean, I've been waiting ALL SEASON for Jake and Ty to reconcile (and really reconcile, not that stupid okay-I-guess-we-can-work-together thing from episode 4…) and now they have. And it was beautiful! The honesty! The empathy! The *hugging*, you guys! I was dancing around my living room!

So imagine my surprise when I got online and found it had managed to upset so many people. Apparently there are viewers of this show who aren't interested in harmonious dynamics between Jake and Ty. I don't get it. Are they watching it for the plot? Because I have some bad news, you guys – the plot's not that strong. If you're looking for shocking twists and great writing, there are absolutely better shows out there. We're in this for character dynamics, right?

Can I ask a question? And I'm being completely sincere about this; I really want to know. To the people who were let down by this week's episode – what would you have rather had happen? Because it's not like anyone was happy a few weeks ago when Jake and Ty were at each other's throats. So I'm confused. What's the solution?

Personally, I couldn't be happier with the show. Maybe I took the "fan" in "fandom" too literally?

Here are some fic recs:
<u>In Boxes</u> – _beautifuleyedea_
<u>Three Days Of Rain</u> – jakety99
<u>Mad World</u> – _EvenIf

>>>>mmmZack reblogged this from finnblueline
>>>>DanniRice reblogged this and added: amen!

>>>>Tylergirl93 reblogged this and added: Tyler shouldn't be
expected to magically forgive Jake for everything he's ever done
after the way Jake's always jerked him around. Ugh, jakegirls.
>>>>slotohes reblogged this from DanniRice
>>>>_EvenIf reblogged this and added: hey :)

**I AM A STICKY NOTE**

Good morning sunshine!
Thanks for not
waking me up :)
best girlfriend.
Bring home crullers
today? xoxo
—Charlie

FROM: US POSTAL SERVICE EMPLOYMENT OFFICE
<CAREERSINMAIL@USPS.GOV>
TO: FINN BARTLETT <FINN.A.BARTLETT@GMAIL.COM>
DATE: MONDAY, FEBRUARY 23 8:02 AM
SUBJECT: APPLICATION FOR EMPLOYMENT

Ms. Bartlett,

Thank you for your interest in the US Postal Service. Although
you meet our qualifications, we have offered the position to a
candidate with more work experience. We wish you the best of
luck in your job search.

FROM: GAVIN MACLEOD <GMACL@SERVSTAR.COM>
TO: FINN BARTLETT <FINN.A.BARTLETT@GMAIL.COM>
DATE: MONDAY, FEBRUARY 23 8:10 AM
SUBJECT: REGRETS

Ms. Bartlett,

Regrettably, all sales positions have been filled. We encourage you to apply with us again in a few months, as something may be available then.

I AM A STICKY NOTE

Ok, where the hell did you find these sticky notes? These are hilarious. Have a good night. Make good tips.
xoxo —Finn

I AM A STICKY NOTE

Finn— I don't work tonight, and there's something I want to talk to you about. Can you come straight home when you get off work?

I AM A STICKY NOTE

Nothing bad, don't worry. I've been doing a lot of thinking about the future — our future — and now that we're living together and you've got your job I thought it

→

I AM A STICKY NOTE

was time we had a conversation about some stuff. I'll get dinner. I love you! Have a GREAT DAY! XXXOOOXXXOOO —Charlie what's with the 911? you okay?

weird note from Charlie this morning

weird how?

I think he might be going to propose

holy shit

yeah

youngest sister gets married first; scandal erupts

oh hush

congratulations! are you excited?

...I don't know

isn't it good news?

*Mar 4, 5:13 pm*

finny?

*Mar 4, 5:16 pm*

guess not.

## TEXT WITH ANGIE

Charlie proposed?? details.

who told you that?

Lydia!

no, he didn't

oh

you might want to call mom

Hey parents.

Apparently there are some rumors going around, so let me clear this up before you get the wrong idea from certain older sisters.

No, Charlie did not propose.

What happened was, he left me a note this morning telling me to come straight home when I got off because he'd been thinking about the future and I freaked out and told Lydia.

It turned out he just wanted to talk about where we're headed, not actually declare any intentions. Which was a relief, because I honestly don't know what I'd have said. I don't want to break up with him, but I have no idea if I could turn down a proposal and still stay with the guy. Is that even allowed?

But anyway, false alarm, nobody's getting married.

We now return you to your regularly scheduled Tuesday.

-Finn

Charlie proposed?

nope, sent you an email

too bad! we were excited for you!

no, it's good, believe me

you don't want to marry him?

not today

then why did you move across the country to be with him?

*Mar 4, 11:11 pm*

---

PRIVATE MESSAGE TO _EvenIf ✕

Hey...

So, stop me if this is weird, but some stuff is happening and I can't really talk to any of my three-dimensional friends about it. Do you mind if I unload a little? I understand if not. I just feel like you get me, or something. Am I crazy? Don't answer that.

-me

hey, of course. what's up?

--genevieve

I don't know how to say this without sounding terrible.

Charlie wants to marry me.

Okay, that needs more explanation. I got home from work today and he'd made this BIG DINNER, like, from a recipe, not our usual pizza and garlic toast, and we ate at the table, which is not something we ever do. And he started making this speech about how long we've been together and how he's never been this happy with anyone...I mean, it was like something out of a cheesy but heartwarming movie.

He didn't propose, but he has this whole timeline in mind of when things should happen, and he asked if I knew my ring size (does anybody know their ring size?).

And my heart just SANK.

I feel so shitty.

I love him.

I really really really do not want to break up with him.

But marriage is a BIG FUCKING DEAL and I just don't KNOW.

...Oh god what if he wanted the extra bedroom for a BABY?

all right, this calls for actual email. ggoldman@stoneyhall.edu.

FROM: FINN BARTLETT <FINN.A.BARTLETT@GMAIL.COM>
TO: GENEVIEVE GOLDMAN <GGOLDMAN@STONEYHALL.EDU>
DATE: TUESDAY, MARCH 4 11:46 PM
SUBJECT: FANCYPANTS

> No shit, Stoneyhall? You are fancy, Genevievie.
>
> Okay. Advise me.

FROM: GENEVIEVE GOLDMAN <GGOLDMAN@STONEYHALL.EDU>
TO: FINN BARTLETT <FINN.A.BARTLETT@GMAIL.COM>
DATE: WEDNESDAY, MARCH 5 2:58 AM
SUBJECT: CHARLIE

> i have no idea what i would do in your shoes. probably break up
> with him, honestly. don't take that as advice.
>
> what's it like living with him? do you want to do it forever? ugh,
> i don't even want to live with my roommate another two months
> and i like her. i can't imagine living with someone forever. i
> honestly want to die alone with some iguanas or something.

FROM: FINN BARTLETT <FINN.A.BARTLETT@GMAIL.COM>
TO: GENEVIEVE GOLDMAN <GGOLDMAN@STONEYHALL.EDU>
DATE: WEDNESDAY, MARCH 5 12:10 AM
SUBJECT: RE: CHARLIE

> The thing is that I don't really KNOW what it's like living with him. I
> work during the day and he works at night. So it's fine, so far, but
> I don't think it would be like this forever at all.
>
> You know what's fucked up? I keep thinking, how can I spend my
> life with someone who doesn't know about fandom? I guess I kind
> of mean it symbolically, but I kind of don't, too. It's this pretty big
> part of my life. Which I guess means I have to tell him. Or else not
> marry him. If I even want to marry him...

FROM: GENEVIEVE GOLDMAN <GGOLDMAN@STONEYHALL.EDU>
TO: FINN BARTLETT <FINN.A.BARTLETT@GMAIL.COM>
DATE: WEDNESDAY, MARCH 5 3:15 AM
SUBJECT: RE: CHARLIE

dude i was just thinking the same thing.

FROM: FINN BARTLETT <FINN.A.BARTLETT@GMAIL.COM>
TO: GENEVIEVE GOLDMAN <GGOLDMAN@STONEYHALL.EDU>
DATE: WEDNESDAY, MARCH 5 12:18 AM
SUBJECT: RE: CHARLIE

You are making me feel so NORMAL right now. Thank you.

FROM: GENEVIEVE GOLDMAN <GGOLDMAN@STONEYHALL.EDU>
TO: FINN BARTLETT <FINN.A.BARTLETT@GMAIL.COM>
DATE: WEDNESDAY, MARCH 5 3:25 AM
SUBJECT: RE: CHARLIE

yeah? i think that's probably the first time anyone's ever said that to me.

i don't know. i've just never met anyone i wanted to actually spend a lot of time with. i mean, i like people, but most of the time i'm with them i'm just waiting for them to leave so i can take off my pants and flop down with my laptop and not have to be anything. i like sneaking out and making out and being totally average outside and then coming back and being my weird version of fandom-famous inside and also just being ALONE. this is sounding really depressing or something but i'm really happy doing this. i've got my life all drawn and quartered.

FROM: FINN BARTLETT <FINN.A.BARTLETT@GMAIL.COM>
TO: GENEVIEVE GOLDMAN <GGOLDMAN@STONEYHALL.EDU>
DATE: WEDNESDAY, MARCH 5 12:31 AM
SUBJECT: RE: CHARLIE

Maybe that's my problem. I'm sure I'll get married SOMEDAY (maybe) but I like having things that are just mine for now. I live in Charlie's house. I hang out with Charlie's friends and family. Mine are all back in Iowa. Fandom is MY thing. I don't know.

# Tylergirl93's
## JOURNAL

......................................................

### -Tyler Pierce has ruined me for life

......................................................

**March 26**

CONVENTION ALERT! This year's *Up Below* con is happening in Chicago and passes are selling for a mint! You will not get one, don't bother trying.

BUT! Through a combination of hard work and good fortune, I've got a lead on an online auction for a set of six passes. Right now the bid's at $600, and these are the GOOD passes, y'all, the ones with the admission to the Q&A session, the afterparty, and you can even get a picture with Toby! (Or Zack, if you're into that.)

Does anyone want to go in on this? Split the cost six ways, if we can get enough people.

### 8 Comments

Leave a comment

**popstotheweasel**
IN.

**Tumbledown**
Um, dates?

> **Tylergirl93**
> First week of July

>> **Tumbledown**
>> No can do, sorry

**Third_The_Bird**
How high do you think the bidding will go?

**Tylergirl93**

No idea. You'd have to commit before we bid it up, though.

**finnblueline**

I'd consider this

**Tylergirl93**

Cool, well, let me know.

FROM: FINN BARTLETT <FINN.A.BARTLETT@GMAIL.COM>
TO: GENEVIEVE GOLDMAN <GGOLDMAN@STONEYHALL.EDU>
DATE: WEDNESDAY, MARCH 26 10:02 PM
SUBJECT: CHICAGO CON?

> Hey, you never told me about your Tylergirl93 drama. Is she
> awful? I don't know if you saw her journal, but she's trying to get
> a group together for the Chicago con, and I could stand to get
> away for a while, but not if she's too unbearable.

FROM: GENEVIEVE GOLDMAN <GGOLDMAN@STONEYHALL.EDU>
TO: FINN BARTLETT <FINN.A.BARTLETT@GMAIL.COM>
DATE: THURSDAY, MARCH 27 1:46 AM
SUBJECT: RE: CHICAGO CON?

> ugh, it's this huge thing. we used to be friends, not like share
> intimate stuff friends, but like talk a bunch every day, do races
> to meet word count goals, whatever. she never learned my real
> name, for whatever that's worth. anyway she decided to have
> this big comment-fic thing--people leave prompts, other people
> come along and write short things, they're a lot of fun--and she
> wanted me to help draw in a crowd since i knew a different set
> of people--jake people. so i brought them in, and you probably
> know that we're this ridiculous minority, but maybe that was
> what had us so amped to be together and we produced a ton of
> shit and it was awesome. we were almost 50/50 for tyler-centric
> and jake-centric. perfect, right?

except then she messages me telling me that, and i am not paraphrasing here, all of the jake fics are MAKING HER SICK because there are so many of them, and this was never supposed to be a jake space and blah blah blah and at first i thought she was blaming me for it, but then i realized what she actually thought was that i was going to just AGREE with her. that underneath i was also thinking that jake fics were making me sick because of course TYLER'S THE ONE WHO'S OBJECTIVELY BETTER.

Like, she thought that i liked jake the way people like store-brand cereal or something. like i picked it because it was easier to grab and it was cheaper, not because i didn't KNOW that the brand-name stuff was better. tyler's lucky charms and jake's that marshmallow hunt in a bag that's one marshmallow for every thousand little frosted hamster food pieces.

well then you know what, mallory? i guess i'm a fucking hamster.

how would you explain going away to charlie, anyway?

FROM: FINN BARTLETT <FINN.A.BARTLETT@GMAIL.COM>
TO: GENEVIEVE GOLDMAN <GGOLDMAN@STONEYHALL.EDU>
DATE: WEDNESDAY, MARCH 26 11:11 PM
SUBJECT: RE: CHICAGO CON?

That was YOU?

Holy shit, I heard about that. A bunch of people were blogging a few months ago about how Jake people take over everything, and someone mentioned that Tylergirl93 (mallory?) had a comment-fic thing going on that she "had to" shut down because people kept posting Jake stories there. The way they described it, it sounded like it had been established specifically for Tyler stories. You're saying she actually invited Jake people and then changed her mind and kicked you out? Wow, that's really pathetic of her.

I think I still want to go to the con though. I've never been to one. And the package is for six people, so maybe somebody cool will go.

Do you ever go to those things?

I'd tell Charlie the truth. I'm not gonna go out of town without telling him where I'm going. I can't be that girl.

FROM: GENEVIEVE GOLDMAN <GGOLDMAN@STONEYHALL.EDU>
TO: FINN BARTLETT <FINN.A.BARTLETT@GMAIL.COM>
DATE: THURSDAY, MARCH 27 2:20 AM
SUBJECT: RE: CHICAGO CON?

are you willing to have that conversation, though? god, i'm making it sound like you're admitting to a murder, i'm sorry. i really don't think it's a big deal. i mean, kids at my school know i write fanfic, but they don't get my username because bitches don't need to know about my profanity problem.

no, i've never been to a con. i know someone who goes to a lot of them who i don't really want to run into. it's a long story. they didn't murder my aunt (she's fine, so) or anything, it would just be kind of awkward. plus aren't those things wicked expensive? i just bought a $300 espresso machine, so i think it might be time to lock my wallet up for this month.

FROM: FINN BARTLETT <FINN.A.BARTLETT@GMAIL.COM>
TO: GENEVIEVE GOLDMAN <GGOLDMAN@STONEYHALL.EDU>
DATE: WEDNESDAY, MARCH 26 11:25 PM
SUBJECT: RE: CHICAGO CON?

It isn't so much that it's a BIG DEAL. I know it's not. But it is a weird hobby, let's call a spade a spade, and the thing is that this is CHARLIE. I don't usually waste a lot of energy worrying about what people think about me, but he's different, you know?

...Okay, I really do have to tell him, don't I.

Oh my god, this is stupid. He's not going to care, right?

How do I explain it to someone who's not part of it, though? Hi, Charlie, guess what, I'm drawing pictures of fictional characters in fantasy situations for my internet friends. It sounds like I'm talking about porn! Oh, hell.

FROM: GENEVIEVE GOLDMAN <GGOLDMAN@STONEYHALL.EDU>
TO: FINN BARTLETT <FINN.A.BARTLETT@GMAIL.COM>
DATE: THURSDAY, MARCH 27 2:27 AM
SUBJECT: RE: CHICAGO CON?

yeah most people who talk about fanfic talk about porn. i'm pretty sure non-fandom people think that's all it is. thanks, 50 shades of grey, appreciate it.

FROM: FINN BARTLETT <FINN.A.BARTLETT@GMAIL.COM>
TO: GENEVIEVE GOLDMAN <GGOLDMAN@STONEYHALL.EDU>
DATE: THURSDAY, MARCH 27 12:23 AM
SUBJECT: OMG

I told him.

FROM: GENEVIEVE GOLDMAN <GGOLDMAN@STONEYHALL.EDU>
TO: FINN BARTLETT <FINN.A.BARTLETT@GMAIL.COM>
DATE: THURSDAY, MARCH 27 3:39 AM
SUBJECT: RE: OMG

tell me everything. (this is not a request. I decided we're at that point.)

FROM: FINN BARTLETT <FINN.A.BARTLETT@GMAIL.COM>
TO: GENEVIEVE GOLDMAN <GGOLDMAN@STONEYHALL.EDU>
DATE: THURSDAY, MARCH 27 12:58 AM
SUBJECT: RE: OMG

It's so awkward right now. I might have made a huge mistake. Fuck.

We were watching last week's episode - Charlie's a casual fan of the show, I have no idea how that's even a thing - and I mentioned that there's a con happening soon. I think he was kind of surprised I knew that, because I'm usually not that plugged in to organized events (I couldn't tell you when ComicCon is happening).

So anyway, he asked if I wanted to go to the con, and I said I'd been thinking about it, and he went and got on his computer and started looking up plane tickets. And there I was thinking I'd completely lucked out, and my boyfriend was a dream come true, and he says -

"It's about $500 for two round trip tickets to Chicago."

He thought I was asking him to come WITH ME. Oh my god, is that something I should have remotely considered? I don't want to be fangirling over Jake with Charlie sitting next to me looking all indulgent (or worse, NOT indulgent) and thinking I'm like that girl who jumped on Toby and practically started having sex with him at that con a few years ago.

(Did that really happen, or is it fandom urban legend?)

So anyway, I said I was thinking about going with some people I knew online, and he got SO judgmental. How did I know these people? Why did I want to go on vacation with random internet people? What if they were actually fifty-year-old rapists?

(Are you actually a fifty-year-old rapist?)

I tried to explain the journaling and the fic writing and the fucking depth with which you know someone, but the truth is, he's right, we DON'T know each other and Tylergirl93 and even you could really be anybody.

Anyway, Charlie's sleeping now and I can't and I have work in two hours. It's going to be a treat.

-me

<u>picture of me</u>

jk that's a picture of a creepy guy i got on google images. <u>this</u> is me actually. note the sign that says "hi finn." and i've skyped with tylergirl, she's a real person. she's even PRETTY, which is just annoying.

i'm so fucking sorry it's awkward. but it'll get better, yeah? maybe you should go to the con with him. get all the awkward out in one hit.

but yeah, that might totally suck.

ugh, real life people.

I don't WANT to go to the con with him. I'd have to pretend to be all casual about the show, and what would be the point?

I think I'm gonna go with the tylergirl group. The price is ridiculously low.

Come? What are the odds you'd run into the person you know? Thousands of people go to these things. I'd love it if there was actually someone I get along with there...

I just realized I might be a 50 year old creeper asking you to meet ME. Attached is a pic of me holding the original of the Mad World drawing I did for you.

FROM: GENEVIEVE GOLDMAN <GGOLDMAN@STONEYHALL.EDU>
TO: FINN BARTLETT <FINN.A.BARTLETT@GMAIL.COM>
DATE: THURSDAY, MARCH 27 4:24 AM
SUBJECT: RE: PHOTO EVIDENCE

i'll definitely consider it...how long do you think i have to decide? i need to look at dates and stuff, i guess.

and i know you're not a creeper, i creeped YOU on facebook the day you told me your last initial. you are, in fact, friends with a creeper. now friend me. Goldman, although I guess you know that from the email address. seriously, how did you not look me up?? you're one of those people who never tried to hack their middle school enemy's email, aren't you.

FROM: FINN BARTLETT <FINN.A.BARTLETT@GMAIL.COM>
TO: GENEVIEVE GOLDMAN <GGOLDMAN@STONEYHALL.EDU>
DATE: THURSDAY, MARCH 27 1:26 AM
SUBJECT: RE: PHOTO EVIDENCE

Creeper! Friended.

The auction ends soon, so we have to decide asap. Pretty please?

FROM: GENEVIEVE GOLDMAN <GGOLDMAN@STONEYHALL.EDU>
TO: FINN BARTLETT <FINN.A.BARTLETT@GMAIL.COM>
DATE: THURSDAY, MARCH 27 4:27 AM
SUBJECT: RE: PHOTO EVIDENCE

I'll think about it.

GENA

**To the graduating seniors of Stoneyhall Preparatory Academy:**

Congratulations on nearing the end of your high school career! We're so proud of all of you, and we're sure the skills you've learned and mastered here at Stoneyhall will lead you toward great success through college and beyond.

We would like to take this opportunity to remind you, however, that the school year is not finished yet! For these next two weeks of exams, please remember to get a lot of sleep and plenty to eat, and, above all, use every scrap of mental energy you have! Remember, you have a nice long summer to recharge before college.

We'd also like to congratulate the following seniors who have already received acceptances to top-tier colleges and universities! Please remember to come sign the wall outside the admissions office—a tradition since Neil Radcliffe was our first student accepted to Harvard in 1932, three years after we were founded.

> **Robert Abandcus** – Princeton University
> **Sophie Balway** – Bromhill University
> **Magnolia Carson** – Lenore College
> **John Cromwell** – Harvard University
> **Eric Doleweather** – Harvard University
> **Genevieve Goldman** – Oakmoor University
> **Maria Jenkings** – Cornell University
> **Alana Jones** – Crestland College
> **Jane Kenwood** – Fairland University
> **Isaac Levine** – Crestland College
> **Keisha Ojukwo** – Yale University
> **Jasper Quentin** – Princeton University
> **Rebekah Samuels** – Stanford University
> **Tamra Tuller** – Harvard University
> **Martin Victor** – Lenore College
> **Christina Xavier** – Harvard University
> **Joshua Zimmerman** – Harvard University

Ⓧ

they spelled my fuckin name
wrong. 7 years, man.

i didn't know levine got
into your school

yea if i lonely-bang him
you have to promise youll
shoot me

lol

best friend obligation

*Apr 9, 6:19 pm*

i'll be in RI girl, im gonna have
to hire a representative to do it

yea but youll come visit all
the time

*Apr 9, 6:26 pm*

yeah of course.

Hey, Bug--

Your aunt told me about Oakmoor! Congrats, kiddo. We're so
proud of you. I bet all you've learned at Stoneyhall's gonna make
you top of your class the first WEEK.

Glad to hear everything's going well! What are you learning in
Chemistry? Rethinking it as a major? It's up to you, Bug, you

know we just want you to do what makes you happy. Still writing your poems?

Off those meds yet?

Keep it up, Bug. Looking forward to talking to you once we've got reliable phone service again. Right now I'm in an Internet cafe in Ruisui Township in Hualien County. Taking lots of pictures! Your mom's out seeing what we haven't tried at the market in central Ruisui. No psychotropic berries yet. :)

Love ya,
Dad

FROM: SETH GOLDMAN <DRJONES.FEDORA@GMAIL.COM>
TO: GENEVIEVE GOLDMAN <GGOLDMAN@STONEYHALL.EDU>
DATE: THURSDAY, APRIL 10 9:02 AM
SUBJECT: RE: (NO SUBJECT)

Hi Dad--

Molarity mostly in Chemistry. It's pretty cool. Did you know that the volume in the equation $C_i = n_i/V$ refers to the volume of the solution, not the volume of the solvent?

Don't really write anything anymore. It's fine. Busy with my friends and stuff. Living it up :)

Bet Ruisui is gorgeous.

Tell Mom I say hi.

Love,
Gena

# ON JOHN'S WALL

I didn't learn a Windsor knot from you.
Your shorts hang off my knees and bite my skin.
The whole of me could not fill up your shoe.
I'm half a boy and half a girl too thin.

You were a boy. I shrunk so you would fit.
I'm angry like it's your fault that you grew
but didn't pause to wash a girl a bit.
You left me huge and threadbare. Bad as new.

If I wear all your clothes and shrivel up,
Will my dresses and my dreams get trapped and die?
Did cutting off my hair make me feel cold?
Did it only make me hard for you to hide?

I try to bare, return the clothes to shelf.
Say, "Half the fun's in lies we tell ourselves."

TEXT WITH JOHN C.

you were a cute 6 year old

*Apr 11, 1:09 pm*

no. shit. you're fucking kidding
me.

i swear i wasn't looking for it.
flipping through the channels
in the lounge looking for
sports and they've been
rerunning on abc family again
looks like

"sports"?? you realize people who actually watch sports generally care about which one

ha yeah, all right, say yes to the dress, sue me

seriously?

nah, cake boss. splitting the difference.

almost liked you there for a second

come down and we'll watch it

ew.

then I guess i'll keep watching little nina tinnerman

timmerman

seriously. You were really fucking cute

still are

creepy

*Apr 11, 1:22 pm*

thanks for giving me that chem anecdote. i'm sure he bought it

*Apr 11, 1:29 pm*

shouldn't you be studying instead of watching old sitcoms?

trying to figure out if you still have that lisp

ugh

*Apr 11, 1:41 pm*

yeah

hey. busy?

kinda. y

any chance you can come over
and distract me? I'm kinda
freaking out about calc final.
And other shit.

*Apr 11, 7:24 pm*

so now you want me.

what?

*Apr 11, 7:29 pm*

wtf?

*Apr 11, 7:42 pm*

is this about last night?

FROM: GENEVIEVE GOLDMAN <GGOLDMAN@STONEYHALL.EDU>
TO: FINN BARTLETT <FINN.A.BARTLETT@GMAIL.COM>
DATE: *NONE. SAVED TO DRAFTS.*
SUBJECT: CON

Hey there Finnegan,

real life sucks. are those convention tickets still an

## TEXT WITH MICHELLE Q.

what do you think the odds are
of someone recognizing my
name?

what?

or face even

what?

*Apr 11, 8:52 PM*

never mind

FROM: GENEVIEVE GOLDMAN <GGOLDMAN@STONEYHALL.EDU>
TO: FINN BARTLETT <FINN.A.BARTLETT@GMAIL.COM>
DATE: FRIDAY, APRIL 11 9:04 PM
SUBJECT: CON

Hey there Finnegan,

real life sucks. are those convention tickets still an option?
i'm so in.

i've attached a photo of a sloth because why not.

Gena

FROM: FINN BARTLETT <FINN.A.BARTLETT@GMAIL.COM>
TO: GENEVIEVE GOLDMAN <GGOLDMAN@STONEYHALL.EDU>
DATE: SATURDAY, APRIL 12 9:32 PM
SUBJECT: CON

Please tell me this is a photo you took yourself.

Actually, tell me all about it IN CHICAGO, girl!!

# Stonenhall Preparatory Academy

This certifies that

*Genevieve Zeporah Goldman*

has completed the course prescribed by the Connecticut State

Board of Education to the standards from which this academy

was founded and is entitled to this

*Diploma*

and has earned all rights and privileges pertaining therein

*This Saturday, May Twenty-First*

*Martin Comback*

**SUPERINTENDENT**

*Jean-Luc Aglion*

**HEAD OF SCHOOL**

part two

# UP̲BELOW

## CONVENTION
### ITINERARY

## JULY 6

**3 pm–7 pm**: Registration/Check-in and receive event passes and gift bag – Hotel Lobby

**9 pm**: Dessert Social (cosplay welcome!) – Main Ballroom

## JULY 7

**9 am**: Breakfast Q&A with Zack and Toby (Gold Badge Holders only) – Lennox Room

**11 am**: Writers' Panel: What's Coming Up in Season 4! – Lincoln Room

**1 pm**: Lunch – Main Ballroom

**2 pm–6 pm**: Exhibit Halls Open

**7 pm**: Dinner – Main Ballroom

**9 pm**: Fan video contest and awards – Lennox Room

## JULY 8

**9 am–12 pm**: Exhibit Halls Open

**1 pm**: Lunch – Main Ballroom

**2 pm–6 pm**: Exhibit Halls Open

**2 pm**: Photo Ops with the Cast (Gold Badge Holders only)– Lennox Room

**4 pm**: Cast and crew autograph signing (Gold Badge Holders only) – Lennox Room

**7 pm**: Dinner – Main Ballroom

## JULY 9

**9 am**: Carl Casden Panel: Ben Evanson, Hero or Villain? – Lincoln Room

**11 am**: Directors' Panel: The Shocking Twists of Season 3

**1 pm**: Lunch – Main Ballroom

**2 pm–6 pm**: Exhibit Halls Open

**2 pm**: RPG Adventure – Hotel Lobby

**4 pm**: Fan art contest and awards – Lennox Room

**7 pm**: Dinner – Main Ballroom

## JULY 10

**9 am**: Breakfast Q&A with Carl Casden (Gold Badge Holders only) – Lennox Room

**11 am**: Zack Martocchio and Toby Frost Panel: Jake and Tyler, Season 3, and What's Ahead for the Guys – Main Ballroom

**1 pm**: Lunch – Lincoln Room

**1 pm**: Private Lunch with Zack and Toby (Gold Badge Holders only) – Lennox Room

**2 pm–6 pm**: Exhibit Halls Open

**7 pm**: Dinner – Main Ballroom

**9 pm**: Cocktails and dancing – Lincoln Room

## JULY 11

**12 pm**: Checkout deadline

⊗

FINN

## TEXT WITH EVIE

tell me i remembered your
number

yes, this is Vlad, and you are?

...

lol hi it's me

are you here??

by the registration table.
it's MOBBED

meet me by the elevators.
yellow dress.

## GROUP TEXT

Mallory: Are y'all here?

Jen: check

check

Sara: about 30 min away

Mallory: HURRY UP
YOU'LL MISS
REGISTRATION

Evie: registration's open for
3 more hrs calm down mal

## TEXT WITH CHARLIE

make it there okay?

all checked in. rm 258 if
you need to call the hotel or
something

miss you

miss you too!

have fun fangirling!

*July 6, 5:42 pm*

thx

you making fun of me?

no!

*July 6, 5:50 pm*

meet any of your internet friends yet?

they seem nice

good!

so not old men then

old men could be nice :p

but in this case no

gotta run, they're texting

love you!

love you

## GROUP TEXT

Sarah: where are we meeting up for the cosplay dessert?

Sarah: I'm dressing as Tyler

Jen: I'm Jake!

Mallory: um, I'M dressing as Tyler

you guys know half the people there are going to be tyler right?

it's okay

Mallory: we need an rpg group. someone has to be evanson

Mallory: sarah be evanson

Sarah: I'm tyler

Mallory: gena, be evanson

Evie: lol no

Mallory: be evanson or you can't be in our cosplay

want to skip the cosplay?

um, yeah.

## TRANSCRIPT EXCERPT: WRITERS' PANEL

**STU WILSON:** What made season 3 so exciting for us as writers was that it was the first time the great bond Ty and Jake share had really been tested. They were both outside their comfort zone, forced to rely on themselves and on other people instead of each other. And that's always a lot of fun, when you get to break convention like that.

**MARIAN LITTLE:** I think we did upset some fans, though.

**SW:** Ha! You could say that. We got some angry letters this season. Particularly after the fire in 3.16. I think there was a feeling that . . . we could have handled that differently.

**[Audience murmur.]**

**ML:** This show has a truly amazing fan base, and we consider it a responsibility to take care of the fans and . . . keep the story something viewers will love. But taking risks is also an important part of what we do, and we hope the fans trust that we do have you in mind.

FROM: FINN BARTLETT <FINN.A.BARTLETT@GMAIL.COM>
TO: CHARLIE THOMAS <DPS.DEALING.BOSS@GMAIL.COM>
DATE: TUESDAY, JULY 8 8:36 PM
SUBJECT: HI FROM CHICAGO!

Hey!

Oh my god, I'm having such a good time. I'm so glad I came.

The girls I'm here with are – well, kind of annoying, to be honest. They talk a lot about how hot Toby Frost is. And, I mean, he is hot, but there isn't a lot to say on the subject. I don't know that they're interested in the characters in the same way I am. I don't know. It makes me feel weird. I guess I thought I'd come out here and feel like I was with My People (and I kind of do) but maybe it's too much to expect that kind of homogeneity from a group of thousands.

The exception is Evie. She's the one who writes the journal I showed you, and she's a RIOT. She's in here now (we're hiding from some of the other girls in our group and watching Up Below and eating a lot of Twizzlers) and she's delivering one of Evanson's speeches right along with him and it's SO DRAMATIC AND HILARIOUS. Maybe it's because her hair's all messed up from sticking her head out the cab window on the way back from the sushi place. I don't know how to explain it. She's great.

(Everyone else calls her Gena, which is pretty funny. She told me that online, but I kept thinking about her as "Eve," and it's just who she is to me now.)

We've all got gold badges, and it's amazing. I got my picture taken with Zack Martocchio, and he signed a picture I drew of him. I think he was really impressed!

Something's kind of weird, though. Evie's been blowing off all the gold pass events. First she skipped the special Q&A with Zack and Toby where you actually get to have a conversation with them (I had to sit with this girl Mallory who's incredibly annoying), and then she didn't even want to go to the photo op. No idea what that's about.

Anyway, thanks for being so great about me coming here. I'm having a blast.

Love you, miss you, see you soon,
-me

FROM: CHARLIE THOMAS <DPS.DEALING.BOSS@GMAIL.COM>
TO: FINN BARTLETT <FINN.A.BARTLETT@GMAIL.COM>
DATE: TUESDAY, JULY 8 7:12 PM
SUBJECT: RE: HI FROM CHICAGO!

Glad you're having such a good time! Where does Evie live? Maybe you two could see each other again after this.

Sounds like she's just not as starstruck as you are. I wouldn't read into it.

Love!
-Charlie

FROM: FINN BARTLETT <FINN.A.BARTLETT@GMAIL.COM>
TO: CHARLIE THOMAS <DPS.DEALING.BOSS@GMAIL.COM>
DATE: TUESDAY, JULY 8 9:40 PM
SUBJECT: RE: HI FROM CHICAGO!

I am NOT STARSTRUCK.

Fuck off :P

-me

**TOBY FROST:** Zack, though . . . Zack has had a long and illustrious career.

**ZACK MARTOCCHIO:** Shut up, dude.

**TF:** What? I'm proud of your work, I can't say that?

**ZM:** You're being a jerk.

**TF:** I'm being a *supportive partner*.

**[Audience laughs.]**

**TF:** Any *Man of the House* fans? God, that was a fun show, wasn't it?

**[Audience cheer.]**

**TF:** Me too. Let's talk about *Man of the House*!

**ZM:** No one's here to talk about *Man of the House*.

**TF:** Dude, you didn't see her?

**ZM:** See who?

**TF:** In the back there. Isn't that Genny Goldman?

**ZM:** . . . Genny?

**[Audience turns to look as girl departs hastily through rear door. A minute later, ZACK follows.]**

**TF:** Uhhh . . . Who wants to hear a story about Carl Casden driving a golf cart into a snack bar?

Mallory: HOW DO YOU KNOW TOBY!

Sara: can you introduce us?

Jen: OMG what just happened?

evie, are you okay?

FROM: FINN BARTLETT <FINN.A.BARTLETT@GMAIL.COM>
TO: CHARLIE THOMAS <DPS.DEALING.BOSS@GMAIL.COM>
DATE: THURSDAY, JULY 10 3:16 PM
SUBJECT: DRAMA

You won't believe what happened today. It's insane.

We were at the Zack and Toby panel (where the stars talk about the show and acting and answer questions from the audience) and some girl asked what they'd be doing if they weren't on Up Below, which led Toby into this tangent about Zack's past acting jobs. You probably know he was the star of Man of the House when we were kids.

But then Toby pointed to the back of the room – I swear, I thought he was pointing at me – and goes, isn't that Genny Goldman? And Evie jumped up like her chair was on fire and ran out of the room. I haven't seen her since.

FROM: CHARLIE THOMAS <DPS.DEALING.BOSS@GMAIL.COM>
TO: FINN BARTLETT <FINN.A.BARTLETT@GMAIL.COM>
DATE: THURSDAY, JULY 10 1:22 PM
SUBJECT: RE: DRAMA

Googled it. Genny Goldman played the little sister on *Man of the House*. Is this her?

...holy shit.

## TEXT WITH EVIE

sorry I took off. mad?

no. come back okay?

have to tell you something.

it's okay, I already know.

*July 10, 8:20 pm*

want to skip the cocktail party?

do we have to talk about it?

not if you don't want to

okay

come to my room

on my way. love ya.

GENA/FINN

**Genevieve:** hey i'm home

or, you know, the illustrious home of my aunt and uncle

**Finn:** me too. not the illustrious aunt and uncle part.

**Genevieve:** they have seven dogs

like, i like dogs

but there's a time and a place

and apparently they've decided that all the times and places are right here and right now.

**Finn:** I see what you mean about illustriousness

**Genevieve:** absolutely
*Sent at 11:05 PM on Tuesday*

**Finn:** So...you doing okay?

**Genevieve:** yeah

it's so weird

i mean i've gone to the same school for almost half my life

being a child star was a big deal for like...three days, seven years ago

**Finn:** he shouldn't have called you out in front of the whole room like that

**Genevieve:** at least it wasn't zack

**Finn:** that was sweet of him to go after you

**Genevieve:** he's always been nice

i can tell you lots of stories now

he took really good care of me. that was kind of a bad time in my life

**Finn:** somewhere mal's shitting herself. I saw her at checkout and she was SO PISSED not to know what's going on

**Genevieve:** ha! i'm sure she'll figure it out.

i don't suppose you remember nina's awkward write-off from man of the house

**Finn:** I remember wondering why she wasn't around anymore. I don't think I ever saw the episode where they explained it

**Genevieve:** it wasn't even a whole episode, it was the five minutes before the first commercial break

they said i went off to beauty school

and zack had this line like "good thing, she needs it!"

laugh track

**Finn:** ...beauty school?

**Genevieve:** right?

**Finn:** you were like four

**Genevieve:** nine, but exactly, makes total sense, right?

anything for a cheap joke

splendid writing on that show. makes up below look emmy worthy

**Finn:** that's shitty

why'd you leave really?

**Genevieve:** hallucinations. plus i stole scissors from wardrobe and cut all my hair off in the boys' dressing room.

no one wants that on set

the crazy, not the chopped-off hair, though someone had to sweep that shit up. i think about that ALL the time. there was a lot of cover up. it would have been really embarrassing for the show, my parents.

**Finn:** that's intense...

**Genevieve:** yeah

i mean, i'm grateful to the show and everything. paid my way through school, let my parents live their dream life of wanderlust

and there's good memories from it

but every time i hear that fucking theme song it's just this reminder of how bad things can get in my head.

**Finn:** you didn't really seem like it was that positive a thing for you

**Genevieve:** when, at the hotel?

i was possibly being overdramatic

**Finn:** I mean, I was worried

**Genevieve:** i know, i'm sorry. i was just caught off guard. you helped

**Finn:** good

**Genevieve:** seriously, thank you so much

i don't really have anyone else to talk to about this right now

alanah's still not speaking to me

**Finn:** what's her problem?

**Genevieve:** ugh, it's so stupid

so we have the same birthday

well, off by a day, but whatever

**Finn:** Birthday Buddies, okay

**Genevieve:** and we've been friends since grade 7

so every year we do a party together

when we were kids it was you know, sleepover in her dorm, truth or dare, all very supervised and all that

and then it became sneaking out getting drunk (her) getting detention (us) all those good things

it's all very...glitter. like just think glitter. everywhere. not coming off.

so she asks me what are we going to do for our birthday next year

and first of all that's november

so it's a long way off

**Finn:** and won't you be at school?

**Genevieve:** exactly

i'll be in rhode island

she'll be in VIRGINIA

**Finn:** well...

I mean, I'm on your side, but those are like five minutes apart, right?

**Genevieve:** what???

no no no

you really do not understand the east coast do you

**Finn:** I understand all the states are postage stamps

teeny little things

**Genevieve:** yes but there are many of them

it's about seven hours

**Finn:** how many states apart?

**Genevieve:** rhode island connecticut new york new jersey pennyslvania delaware maryland virginia

**Finn:** LOL! eight states in eight hours

**Genevieve:** it's like you think we have some complex about being small states

this does not bother us

**Finn:** no, it's adorable. good for you

**Genevieve:** you suck

**Finn:** you love me

**Genevieve:** MAYBE

so anyway that's pretty much all i say

seven hours

and she's all

"you mean you aren't going to throw me a party?"

and when this became ME throwing HER a party is anyone's guess

anyway it turned into this whole thing about me thinking my school was better than hers or something?

**Finn:** is it?

**Genevieve:** well yeah, but i didn't know that was something she cared about

but now she's turning it into this whole thing, saying i don't care if she has a party because i think she's just going to a party school anyway

and then she threw up on my shoes

which is why i had to wear those ugly ones all over con

**Finn:** ...I think I missed something here

**Genevieve:** so do i.

**Finn:** I'm sorry

that really sucks

**Genevieve:** i mean...whatever. she's a child.

she's always going to be a child, i guess.

So, you know, college, bigger and better.

**Finn:** talk to her. maybe she's ashamed of herself and can't figure out how to say it

**Genevieve:** yeah. i wanted to talk to her about con all week. tell someone anyway.

can i tell you something dumb?

**Finn:** uh huh

**Genevieve:** i got so jealous when you kept emailing charlie

just like...wishing i had someone to tell stuff to, i guess

**Finn:** can I tell you something dumb?

**Genevieve:** even before we fought i didn't talk about anything serious with alanah or anythng

yeah

**Finn:** I was emailing him about you

**Genevieve:** no shit

what did you say??

was it about my nose because i'm gonna get it fixed someday

who am i kidding i'm totally not

me and schnoz, til death do us part

**Finn:** yeah, don't do that. look what happened to your beloved jennifer grey

**Genevieve:** ugh, i should be so lucky

**Finn:** said the famous actress who's worked with ZACK MARTOCCHIO

**Genevieve:** yeah that's what i'm saying, it'd be nice to pull a jenn and disappear

i met her once actually

**Finn:** SHUT UP

**Genevieve:** yeah i don't remember though

but i have a picture with her. my mom says i cried

**Finn:** were you little?

**Genevieve:** yeah, five or six

i left the show when i was nine, haven't done anything since then

my agent emails me sometimes

**Finn:** yeah? do you ever think about getting back into it?

**Genevieve:** no

i like my life

**Finn:** cool

**Genevieve:** i'm gonna be a child psychologist and go around slapping parents who try to put their kids in show business

**Finn:** so it's gotta be weird, right?

I mean...jakegirling when you kind of know zack

**Genevieve:** oh god it's so weird you have no idea

have i told you how i saw my first episode?

**Finn:** no

**Genevieve:** this girl lea, a year older than me, graduated, went to sarah lawrence, etc

she was my math tutor and i go to her dorm and she's like hey come in my show's just finishing up

and it's mid-season one, you know that ep where jake's undercover as the fireman? lol this show i can not even sometimes

**Finn:** oh, the one when he had the scratch under his eye?

**Genevieve:** yeah. we're so normal.

anyway this was post-scratch though, the part when he was in the helmet for the rest of the ep

**Finn:** okay

**Genevieve:** and he was barely in the last few scenes, it was mostly tyler and nicola

**Finn:** ewww nicola

**Genevieve:** i know i don't know why that didn't turn me off it immediately

but it didn't, and i was kind of into it and the next week i went to her dorm a little early so i could see more of it oh and i'd been reading fanfic that whole week because obviously

**Finn:** so wait

you were reading fic without having seen a whole episode?

**Genevieve:** yes

**Finn:** awesome, go on

**Genevieve:** i really like fic, lol

so i go over to her dorm

and THAT'S WHEN I FIND OUT IT'S ZACK.

and i'm like oh jesus COME ON.

but at that point it was too late, y'know?

so i just try to disconnect them a LOT

but yeah it's really awkward because i'm all...oh my god jake you're in pain let me hold you

and in my head i'm like yep, that's what zack ACTUALLY LOOKS LIKE when he cries.

**Finn:** ...is it bad that I love knowing that

**Genevieve:** do you think i told you for no reason?

**Finn:** you're fantastic

**Genevieve:** thank you dear

he's a good guy. but it's still so weird sometimes

like when jakegirls go on and on about how hot he is

it's like GROSS THAT'S MY BROTHER

but at the same time he's so hot so like fuck my life all over

anyway when stuff started to get really bad for me he took care of me

he's just a good guy

i think zack could tell before anyone

**Finn:** yeah?

what was it like?

**Genevieve:** it's like everything goes dark

not like literally dark

you can still see but there's something about it telling you that it's not important that nothing is important

you're just in this black and white box of...never mattering

and then there are these voices and these animals that don't look like animals and they're SO bright

or something. it's been a long time.

anyway what I remember the most because like, it's so embarrassing in retrospect

i used to hallucinate fires all the time, like i'd be on set and i'd just think things were on fire

i was so much fucking trouble because i was always freaking out and i'd pull fire alarms and drench the studio and shit when there was nothing wrong and everyone thought i was just being a brat

i'd just see fire everywhere

anyway after a while it became clear i was kind of a mess and a lawsuit waiting to happen, tbh, and the producers said the show was going to go in a different direction

but then the show was gone, and my routine was gone, and my friends were gone, and then it just...

i don't really know how to talk about it.

**Finn:** you don't have to

**Genevieve:** i'm sorry.

**Finn:** no, I'm sorry

**Genevieve:** i know this isn't fun to listen to

my friends here all get uncomfortable

**Finn:** hey, no, it's not like that

I don't want to push you into talking about something so hard, is all

**Genevieve:** maybe it wouldn't be so hard anymore if i'd gotten to talk about it, you know?

**Finn:** yeah

**Genevieve:** all my parents ever say about it is are you off the meds yet

that's practically all my fucking psychiatrist says about it

and my friends, whenever one of them is like "wow my bio teacher is a psycho" they're all shutting their mouths and looking at me out of the sides of their eyes like i'm going to burst into tears or something

because apparently it would be fine with them if I were that badly adjusted, but i'm not allowed to talk about it like it's not a big deal. which it's not, really, anymore. it was a long time ago.

so i just don't talk about it at all

which is fine.

**Finn:** well...I wouldn't pretend to know how to help, really, or what the right things to say are

but I'm good at listening

I care about you. if that's not too weird

so...if you ever need anything

and if you just want to talk about jake being perfect, I'm always up for that too
    *Sent at 11:54 PM on Tuesday*

**Genevieve:** heh.

i like you.

**Finn:** I like you too.

**Genevieve:** how's stuff with charlie?

**Finn:** all quiet on the western front

no marriage talk lately

**Genevieve:** and how do you feeeeel about that

**Finn:** lol. relieved. maybe I'm off the hook

**Genevieve:** fingers crossed

how's he doing with fandom stuff?
    *Sent at 11:58 PM on Tuesday*

**Finn:** a lot of jokes at my expense

it's like he's accepting it as long as he gets to mock me a little

it's not mean spirited, so I'll take it

**Genevieve:** go you

:)

all right apparently i have to go walk a dog now

HOLY SHIT no wait

finn holy shit

**Finn:** what?!

**Genevieve:** i have an email from zack

**Finn:** FUCK ME. details.

**Genevieve:** i haven't opened it yet i'm scared

...what the fuck am i scared of

oh my god finn do you know what i'm doing right now

**Finn:** aaaah I have to go to work TEXT ME

**Genevieve:** i'm having a mother fucking FANGIRL MOMENT OVER ZACK MARTOCCHIO

genevieve what have you come to

okay go to work i'll forward it to you

text you asap

xoxo

**Finn:** xxxoo

GENA/ZACK

Hey there, Genevieve--

Kyle gave me your email. I hope that's cool? I meant to get your info at the convention but it was hella hectic.

Toby feels like an ass for pointing you out like that. Trust me, I made sure of it. I think he thought you were there to be noticed. Clearly he didn't ask me about it beforehand. I would have told him no one had heard from you in ages.

Not to mention that even back then you wouldn't let anyone call you Genny.

Are you okay?
-Z

FROM: Genevieve Goldman <genazeporah@gmail.com>
TO: Zack Martocchio <zackm@upbelow.com>
DATE: Thursday, July 17 1:00 PM
SUBJECT: Me too :(

Hi.

I'm okay. Embarrassed mostly about causing a scene and pulling you away like that.

Also embarrassed about being a dorky fangirl over your show.

FROM: Zack Martocchio <zackm@upbelow.com>
TO: Genevieve Goldman <genazeporah@gmail.com>
DATE: Thursday, July 17 1:11 PM
SUBJECT: <3

I love dorky fangirls of my show.

You know people ask me all the time about you.

FROM: GENEVIEVE GOLDMAN <GENAZEPORAH@GMAIL.COM>
TO: ZACK MARTOCCHIO <ZACKM@UPBELOW.COM>
DATE: THURSDAY, JULY 17 1:15 PM
SUBJECT: RE: <3

Who?

FROM: ZACK MARTOCCHIO <ZACKM@UPBELOW.COM>
TO: GENEVIEVE GOLDMAN <GENAZEPORAH@GMAIL.COM>
DATE: THURSDAY, JULY 17 1:18 PM
SUBJECT: RE: <3

Mia, Katherine, Tyson, Carter. And those are just the ones I'm still in touch with.

FROM: GENEVIEVE GOLDMAN <GENAZEPORAH@GMAIL.COM>
TO: ZACK MARTOCCHIO <ZACKM@UPBELOW.COM>
DATE: THURSDAY, JULY 17 1:21 PM
SUBJECT: RE: <3

yeah i saw that reunion special with you guys five years ago. Pretty cute. Nice hair back then, by the way.

FROM: ZACK MARTOCCHIO <ZACKM@UPBELOW.COM>
TO: GENEVIEVE GOLDMAN <GENAZEPORAH@GMAIL.COM>
DATE: THURSDAY, JULY 17 1:22 PM
SUBJECT: :$

Oh god, that was the fauxhawk stage wasn't it?

FROM: GENEVIEVE GOLDMAN <GENAZEPORAH@GMAIL.COM>
TO: ZACK MARTOCCHIO <ZACKM@UPBELOW.COM>
DATE: THURSDAY, JULY 17 1:23 PM
SUBJECT: XD

yeah, you were a walking boy band.

FROM: ZACK MARTOCCHIO <ZACKM@UPBELOW.COM>
TO: GENEVIEVE GOLDMAN <GENAZEPORAH@GMAIL.COM>
DATE: THURSDAY, JULY 17 1:24 PM
SUBJECT: <:-|

I seriously thought of you when they gave me that haircut. And the one in UB season two.

FROM: GENEVIEVE GOLDMAN <GENAZEPORAH@GMAIL.COM>
TO: ZACK MARTOCCHIO <ZACKM@UPBELOW.COM>
DATE: THURSDAY, JULY 17 1:25 PM
SUBJECT: XD XD XD

don't even talk about that i'm laughing too hard to type.

FROM: ZACK MARTOCCHIO <ZACKM@UPBELOW.COM>
TO: GENEVIEVE GOLDMAN <GENAZEPORAH@GMAIL.COM>
DATE: THURSDAY, JULY 17 1:27 PM
SUBJECT: ;)

I seriously looked at myself in the mirror and was like...This is exactly the kind of thing Gena would lose her shit over.

FROM: GENEVIEVE GOLDMAN <GENAZEPORAH@GMAIL.COM>
TO: ZACK MARTOCCHIO <ZACKM@UPBELOW.COM>
DATE: THURSDAY, JULY 17 1:28 PM
SUBJECT: :-0

I kind of can't believe you still think about me. God i'm being such a loser right now. Omg jake thinks about me! I can't believe myself.

FROM: ZACK MARTOCCHIO <ZACKM@UPBELOW.COM>
TO: GENEVIEVE GOLDMAN <GENAZEPORAH@GMAIL.COM>
DATE: THURSDAY, JULY 17 1:34 PM
SUBJECT: :-/

Did they even invite you to that reunion?

FROM: GENEVIEVE GOLDMAN <GENAZEPORAH@GMAIL.COM>
TO: ZACK MARTOCCHIO <ZACKM@UPBELOW.COM>
DATE: THURSDAY, JULY 17 1:40 PM
SUBJECT: :P

louis left a message. i never answered and they never followed up.

FROM: ZACK MARTOCCHIO <ZACKM@UPBELOW.COM>
TO: GENEVIEVE GOLDMAN <GENAZEPORAH@GMAIL.COM>
DATE: THURSDAY, JULY 17 1:58 PM
SUBJECT: :(

> Hey, Gena, do you hate me?

FROM: GENEVIEVE GOLDMAN <GENAZEPORAH@GMAIL.COM>
TO: ZACK MARTOCCHIO <ZACKM@UPBELOW.COM>
DATE: THURSDAY, JULY 17 2:04 PM
SUBJECT: RE: :(

> hey, what?? did you miss the part where i just paid twenty
> thousand dollars to stand in a crowd of sweaty girls screaming
> your name?

FROM: ZACK MARTOCCHIO <ZACKM@UPBELOW.COM>
TO: GENEVIEVE GOLDMAN <GENAZEPORAH@GMAIL.COM>
DATE: THURSDAY, JULY 17 2:10 PM
SUBJECT: RE: :(

> I did that reunion without you. And I never came and found you.

FROM: GENEVIEVE GOLDMAN <GENAZEPORAH@GMAIL.COM>
TO: ZACK MARTOCCHIO <ZACKM@UPBELOW.COM>
DATE: THURSDAY, JULY 17 2:15 PM
SUBJECT: RE: :(

> didn't want to be found. we moved away, i got stuffed with meds
> and shipped off to boarding school. fresh new start and all that,
> everyone gets to wash their hands of it.

FROM: ZACK MARTOCCHIO <ZACKM@UPBELOW.COM>
TO: GENEVIEVE GOLDMAN <GENAZEPORAH@GMAIL.COM>
DATE: THURSDAY, JULY 17 2:22 PM
SUBJECT: RE: :(

> Maybe if I'd done a better job it wouldn't have gotten that bad
> and you could have stayed.

FROM: GENEVIEVE GOLDMAN <GENAZEPORAH@GMAIL.COM>
TO: ZACK MARTOCCHIO <ZACKM@UPBELOW.COM>
DATE: THURSDAY, JULY 17 2:24 PM
SUBJECT: RE: :(

> a better job at what?

FROM: GENEVIEVE GOLDMAN <GENAZEPORAH@GMAIL.COM>
TO: ZACK MARTOCCHIO <ZACKM@UPBELOW.COM>
DATE: THURSDAY, JULY 17 2:24 PM
SUBJECT: RE: :(

> Taking care of you. You know. Little sister.

FROM: GENEVIEVE GOLDMAN <GENAZEPORAH@GMAIL.COM>
TO: ZACK MARTOCCHIO <ZACKM@UPBELOW.COM>
DATE: THURSDAY, JULY 17 2:29 PM
SUBJECT: :)

> ughhh don't get all sad, I can like FEEL you doing that look you
> did when tyler was telling you how he got beat up in prison.
>
> it doesn't work that way. it's a chemical thing. it's bigger than us.

FROM: ZACK MARTOCCHIO <ZACKM@UPBELOW.COM>
TO: GENEVIEVE GOLDMAN <GENAZEPORAH@GMAIL.COM>
DATE: THURSDAY, JULY 17 2:38 PM
SUBJECT: RE: :)

> I told myself you didn't watch the show. The new one.

FROM: GENEVIEVE GOLDMAN <GENAZEPORAH@GMAIL.COM>
TO: ZACK MARTOCCHIO <ZACKM@UPBELOW.COM>
DATE: THURSDAY, JULY 17 2:39 PM
SUBJECT: RE: :)

> Why?

FROM: ZACK MARTOCCHIO <ZACKM@UPBELOW.COM>
TO: GENEVIEVE GOLDMAN <GENAZEPORAH@GMAIL.COM>
DATE: THURSDAY, JULY 17 2:46 PM
SUBJECT: (NO SUBJECT)

> I didn't want to think of you having to look at me.

FROM: GENEVIEVE GOLDMAN <GENAZEPORAH@GMAIL.COM>
TO: ZACK MARTOCCHIO <ZACKM@UPBELOW.COM>
DATE: THURSDAY, JULY 17 2:52 PM
SUBJECT: RE: (NO SUBJECT)

> Fuck, Zack.

FROM: ZACK MARTOCCHIO <ZACKM@UPBELOW.COM>
TO: GENEVIEVE GOLDMAN <GENAZEPORAH@GMAIL.COM>
DATE: THURSDAY, JULY 17 2:55 PM
SUBJECT: RE: (NO SUBJECT)

> You were miserable. Even if I didn't get what that meant and why you were seeing whatever it was you were seeing, I should have done something to make you less miserable.

FROM: GENEVIEVE GOLDMAN <GENAZEPORAH@GMAIL.COM>
TO: ZACK MARTOCCHIO <ZACKM@UPBELOW.COM>
DATE: THURSDAY, JULY 17 2:59 PM
SUBJECT: :P

> seeing fire, mostly. and you were a kid. And you made me glitter glue cards.

FROM: ZACK MARTOCCHIO <ZACKM@UPBELOW.COM>
TO: GENEVIEVE GOLDMAN <GENAZEPORAH@GMAIL.COM>
DATE: THURSDAY, JULY 17 3:04 PM
SUBJECT: RE: :P

> Right, and childhood means blissful innocence.
>
> I should have stepped up.

FROM: GENEVIEVE GOLDMAN <GENAZEPORAH@GMAIL.COM>
TO: ZACK MARTOCCHIO <ZACKM@UPBELOW.COM>
DATE: THURSDAY, JULY 17 3:08 PM
SUBJECT: RE: :P

i love your show.

i love seeing you.

i love the stupid fucking plots, what are you guys even doing half the time.

FROM: ZACK MARTOCCHIO <ZACKM@UPBELOW.COM>
TO: GENEVIEVE GOLDMAN <GENAZEPORAH@GMAIL.COM>
DATE: THURSDAY, JULY 17 3:12 PM
SUBJECT: RE: :P

One of the writers is getting fired next season. Shhh.

FROM: GENEVIEVE GOLDMAN <GENAZEPORAH@GMAIL.COM>
TO: ZACK MARTOCCHIO <ZACKM@UPBELOW.COM>
DATE: THURSDAY, JULY 17 3:13 PM
SUBJECT: RE: :P

god, i miss on-set gossip like crack.

FROM: ZACK MARTOCCHIO <ZACKM@UPBELOW.COM>
TO: GENEVIEVE GOLDMAN <GENAZEPORAH@GMAIL.COM>
DATE: THURSDAY, JULY 17 3:16 PM
SUBJECT: RE: :P

How's Naomi and Seth?

FROM: GENEVIEVE GOLDMAN <GENAZEPORAH@GMAIL.COM>
TO: ZACK MARTOCCHIO <ZACKM@UPBELOW.COM>
DATE: THURSDAY, JULY 17 3:18 PM
SUBJECT: RE: :P

currently hiking some west african trails.

FROM: ZACK MARTOCCHIO <ZACKM@UPBELOW.COM>
TO: GENEVIEVE GOLDMAN <GENAZEPORAH@GMAIL.COM>
DATE: THURSDAY, JULY 17 3:19 PM
SUBJECT: RE: :P

Sounds like them.

So they never pushed you into doing anything else?

FROM: GENEVIEVE GOLDMAN <GENAZEPORAH@GMAIL.COM>
TO: ZACK MARTOCCHIO <ZACKM@UPBELOW.COM>
DATE: THURSDAY, JULY 17 3:21 PM
SUBJECT: HAHA

> my shrink would have killed them.

FROM: ZACK MARTOCCHIO <ZACKM@UPBELOW.COM>
TO: GENEVIEVE GOLDMAN <GENAZEPORAH@GMAIL.COM>
DATE: THURSDAY, JULY 17 3:23 PM
SUBJECT: >:)

> Probably shrinks should kill all showbiz parents.

FROM: GENEVIEVE GOLDMAN <GENAZEPORAH@GMAIL.COM>
TO: ZACK MARTOCCHIO <ZACKM@UPBELOW.COM>
DATE: THURSDAY, JULY 17 3:25 PM
SUBJECT: *\0/*

> ha, i was just telling my best friend how i'm essentially majoring in
> that. Starting college in the fall.

FROM: ZACK MARTOCCHIO <ZACKM@UPBELOW.COM>
TO: GENEVIEVE GOLDMAN <GENAZEPORAH@GMAIL.COM>
DATE: THURSDAY, JULY 17 3:26 PM
SUBJECT: :D

> NICE. Excited?

FROM: GENEVIEVE GOLDMAN <GENAZEPORAH@GMAIL.COM>
TO: ZACK MARTOCCHIO <ZACKM@UPBELOW.COM>
DATE: THURSDAY, JULY 17 3:27 PM
SUBJECT: :DDDDD

> Ridiculously.

FROM: ZACK MARTOCCHIO <ZACKM@UPBELOW.COM>
TO: GENEVIEVE GOLDMAN <GENAZEPORAH@GMAIL.COM>
DATE: THURSDAY, JULY 17 3:29 PM
SUBJECT: 0/\0

> So you really are out.

FROM: GENEVIEVE GOLDMAN <GENAZEPORAH@GMAIL.COM>
TO: ZACK MARTOCCHIO <ZACKM@UPBELOW.COM>
DATE: THURSDAY, JULY 17 3:30 PM
SUBJECT: RE: o/\o

> Really really.

FROM: ZACK MARTOCCHIO <ZACKM@UPBELOW.COM>
TO: GENEVIEVE GOLDMAN <GENAZEPORAH@GMAIL.COM>
DATE: THURSDAY, JULY 17 3:33 PM
SUBJECT: :D

> You don't ever miss it? Fucking happy for you, Genevieve.

FROM: GENEVIEVE GOLDMAN <GENAZEPORAH@GMAIL.COM>
TO: ZACK MARTOCCHIO <ZACKM@UPBELOW.COM>
DATE: THURSDAY, JULY 17 3:39 PM
SUBJECT: RE: :D

> you know what i wish? And it's dumb as shit.

FROM: ZACK MARTOCCHIO <ZACKM@UPBELOW.COM>
TO: GENEVIEVE GOLDMAN <GENAZEPORAH@GMAIL.COM>
DATE: THURSDAY, JULY 17 3:42 PM
SUBJECT: >;)

> Is it an autograph because I can make that happen.

FROM: GENEVIEVE GOLDMAN <GENAZEPORAH@GMAIL.COM>
TO: ZACK MARTOCCHIO <ZACKM@UPBELOW.COM>
DATE: THURSDAY, JULY 17 3:44 PM
SUBJECT: o_o

> dick.

FROM: ZACK MARTOCCHIO <ZACKM@UPBELOW.COM>
TO: GENEVIEVE GOLDMAN <GENAZEPORAH@GMAIL.COM>
DATE: THURSDAY, JULY 17 3:45 PM
SUBJECT: RE: o_o

> Tell me.

that i could act every once in a while without being an ACTOR. like there'd somehow be a way for me to go back and do something without looking like some desperate washed-up child star. sometimes i have to fight the urge to audition for a fucking paper towel commercial or go play a baby-murderer in a law and order episode.

i want to show everyone that i can do it without going crazy and pulling fire alarms or whatever.

really i wish i'd done the fucking reunion show.

This might be the most horrible suggestion in the world, and I would understand if you wanted to get on a plane and come punch me, but...fuck it, you know?

How about just one episode?

GENA

## \_EvenIf's JOURNAL

I watch a lot of *Up Below* and write a lot of fanfic and shoot a lot of heroin. One of those is false. I do a mean French braid.

# Back From the Dead (with fic!)

Jesus mephitis mephitis that was a long absence. SORRY INTERNET. I'm alive. Hopefully I've not been forgotten?

I'm off to college in a few weeks, and I have some other stuff going on out in meatspace as well, but my big news of the summer was that I got to go to Chicago Con!! It was phenomenal beyond all reason. The boys were as charming and eloquent as always and the writers got me so fucking excited about next season.

EXCITED ENOUGH TO WRITE A FANTASY SEASON 4 PREMIERE FIC, you may ask?

YES, I may answer! At least a smidgen of one. So YES, I may WHISPER.

**Title:** Marzipan and Metal Cans

**Author:** \_EvenIf

**Word Count:** 463

**Summary:** Remember that one time we got to see them shop for supplies? That was nice. Let's do that again.

**Pairing:** none, you know what journal you're on.

**Disclaimer:** I own nothing besides my little conference badge.

**Author's Note:** Go easy on me, it's been a tough couple of weeks. Almost out of here. Eve to College, come in, College. College, do you read me?

Jake's on his hands and knees like a damn child, half of him sticking out of a box like it's fucking Christmas morning and Tyler bought him a Red Rider BB gun. "There's nothing in here."

"Well there's about eight hundred things out here, so stop embarrassing us." Tyler picks up a decimated flare gun from the 80% OFF table. What the hell were normal people doing with this flare gun? He's struck again by the fact that he has virtually no idea what normal people do. It's been too long.

Jake emerges with a streak of dust on his cheek and something tiny raised triumphantly over his head.

"The hell is that?"

"Tonka truck."

"You're shitting me."

Jake throws it at him. "Zippo."

"Oh, man." Tyler flicks the wheel with his thumb, watches the flame glow, disappear, glow again.

"My dad had one just like that," Jake says, like it's nothing, like it's no big deal.

Tyler waits for him because maybe this time he'll really talk about what happened the night Alan Henry sunk under the water and never came back. But Jake doesn't say anything more. So Tyler says, "You think we could rehabilitate this thing?"

"Why?"

For setting baddies on fire, numbskull. "For waking you up when you're snoring. KaPOW."

"You're never gonna let that go, are you? I was *sick*. It was either snore or suffocate."

"And you chose the one that keeps you around to piss me off for the rest of my life."

"You're so full of shit."

"Most days." He grabs Jake by the shoulder and pulls him off the ground. "You want to hit on the housewife while we're here?"

Jake cranes his neck around Tyler's shoulder to check out the harried little blonde restocking the table. Yeah, Tyler knows his type. "Yes."

"Get on it, kiddo. I'm gonna check out the bullet situation."

"Oh yeah, I'm sure there's a ton on sale here."

"Need a new jacket?"

"Yes please."

"I'll grab one."

Jake goes over to embarrass himself hitting on a woman in front of her husband (Tyler needed to torture him a bit; it was getting a little sentimental back there) and Tyler leafs through the hunting jackets that will probably never see the outside of an RV. He plays with the lighter while he works, rubbing the wheel back and forth and turning it over and over in his hand.

It's during one of those turns that he sees the initials carved roughly into the bottom, by someone dumb and reckless enough to risk breaking a knife getting them in there (someone dumb and reckless enough to drown while his baby watched).

A. H.

Tyler swallows, slips the lighter into his pocket, and watches Jake be happy, for a little while.

## 24 Comments

Leave a comment

**BlossomButtercup**

He totally didn't pay for that lighter! Awesome job. :)

> **_EvenIf**
>
> That scoundrel!

**SwingLowMySweet**

Oh my God I need this like blood. I'm glad to hear SOMEONE hasn't forgotten we still need Jake's dad resolved *glares at writers*

> **_EvenIf**
>
> gaaaah I know it kills me.

> > **SwingLowMySweet**
> >
> > It was one of my favorite mysteries of s1, what the hell he was looking for under the water, if he had any idea how risky it would be, if he even KNEW THERE WAS SUPPOSED TO BE A SEA MONSTER, I mean, it seems like he MUST have, right?

> > > **_EvenIf**
> > >
> > > I have no idea. as much as I don't want to believe he'd take that risk with Jake RIGHT THERE, he was so committed to proving monsters weren't real...

> > > > **SwingLowMySweet**
> > > >
> > > > Oh poor guy. No idea he was on a TV show.

> > > > > **_EvenIf**
> > > > >
> > > > > People really need to consider that more often.

**CalmMyLightsaber**

Was Tyler trying to burn himself??

> **_EvenIf**
>
> oh who knows with that boy.

> > **CalmMyLightsaber**
> >
> > oh and I loved this

> > > **_EvenIf**
> > >
> > > thank you!!

**finnblueline**

You're pretty.

**_EvenIf**

your FACE is pretty.

**slotohes**

oh my god I so hope this happens

**_EvenIf**

me tooo (obviously) but I should really know better than to get my hopes up at this point. But the stuff they said at the con made me uncomfortably hopeful that we're in for a good season...

**finnblueline**

Oh and fyi the reason you're pretty is because you mentioned when Jake was sick.

**_EvenIf**

NEVER FORGET

**SwingLowMySweet**

You guys are crazy.

**_EvenIf**

you love it like candy.

**TylerGirl93**

This is seriously all you have to say?

**finnblueline**

lol.

**Percymaxon**

love this!!

**_EvenIf**

thank you!

FINN

////////////////////////////////////////////////////////////////

August 8th

//////////////////

All right.

I'm gonna start with the season 3 finale, even though I know I'm a couple weeks late (sorry, sorry!) and it's been hashed to death by now. You know me. I have to have my say.

Guys, that was *amazing*!

That final scene in the warehouse. My GOD. I really didn't think Jake was going to make it out this time! What's happening to me?! Someone says that every week and I always give them a hard time, but I swear, I was *pulling up tufts of carpet* I was so tense. HOLY SHIT. And then Tyler kicked the door in and just... the *feelings*, you guys, the *feelings*.

So season 4 is set up really well, I think, given Evanson's double-cross (which I don't buy for a fucking second, come on, it's EVANSON, there's got to be something behind it) and I can't wait to see where they're taking it.

And I love Jake, but we knew that.

Okay, in other, bigger news...

CHICAGO CON. Whoa. I had no idea it would be so awesome. Zack and Toby are so funny together. I love how close they are in real life. It's like they actually have that whole history together. Which I guess in a way they do. Plus, getting to meet and bond with people I've already gotten to know online was cool, and I'm happy to report that none of you are old-school internet creeps.

So, the moral of this post is, get yourself to a con AQAP, and in the meantime, watch the S3 finale often and GET EXCITED for October. We're in for a hell of a premiere!

And this isn't exactly public knowledge yet, but I just got an insider tip (lol, I'm an insider!) about a guest star you guys won't believe.

Here's a scan of my drawing (signed by Zack!)

>>>>DanniRice reblogged this from finnblueline
>>>>Tylergirl93 reblogged this and added: When at con did any bonding happen? You were hiding out in your room the whole time.
>>>>finnblueline: HANGING out in my room. Important distinction
>>>>_EvenIf: :D
>>>>mmmZack reblogged this from finnblueline
>>>>slotohes reblogged this from DanniRice
>>>>_EvenIf reblogged this and added: LOLOL BEST EVER.

FROM: GENEVIEVE GOLDMAN <GENAZEPORAH@GMAIL.COM>
TO: FINN BARTLETT <FINN.A.BARTLETT@GMAIL.COM>
DATE: FRIDAY, AUGUST 8 10:10 PM
SUBJECT: NERD

haha your journal. "guest star you guys won't believe"? They're going to be thinking it's Demi Lovato or something. No one gives a shit about seeing me on the show, weirdo.

FROM: FINN BARTLETT <FINN.A.BARTLETT@GMAIL.COM>
TO: GENEVIEVE GOLDMAN <GENAZEPORAH@GMAIL.COM>
DATE: FRIDAY, AUGUST 8 7:24 PM
SUBJECT: NERD!

MY BEST FRIEND'S GOING TO BE ON UP BELOW AAAAAAHHHH!

-F

p.s. Who the fuck is Demi Lovato?

FROM: JEAN PARKER <JPARKER@WINDSORHOUSE.COM>
TO: FINN BARTLETT <FINN.A.BARTLETT@GMAIL.COM>
DATE: SATURDAY, AUGUST 9 2:02 PM
SUBJECT: OFFER OF EMPLOYMENT

Ms. Bartlett,

After reviewing your application, we are pleased to offer you the position of data entry technician with Windsor Publishing House. Please call 800-555-2385 and ask for Jean Parker to discuss the terms of employment and arrange your start date. We look forward to you joining our staff!

TEXT WITH CHARLIE (DELETED)

holy shit I

holy shit I just got a job offer

*Aug 9, 2:12 pm*

just saw this. omg. tell.

data entry thing, no big deal, but SALARY AND BENEFITS

paying my share of the rent

plane ticket to RI? lol

don't even joke that would be amazing

*Aug 9, 2:20*

what did charlie say!

haven't told him

why?

it's stupid

no, why?

it's gonna bring up the marriage thing again

we agreed to table it while we were poor

fuck

yeah

you have to tell him

*Aug 9, 2:28 pm*

yeah

# *Rosemont Flowers*

(800) 555-2684

## CONGRATULATIONS!
Finnegan,

good luck at the new job, rock star.
see you in RI soon??

xoxo
Genevievie

FROM: FINN BARTLETT <FINN.A.BARTLETT@GMAIL.COM>
TO: GENEVIEVE GOLDMAN <GENAZEPORAH@GMAIL.COM>
DATE: MONDAY, AUGUST 11 8:40 PM
SUBJECT: CHARLIE ISSUES

Hey, kid.

Thanks for the flowers.

And, holy fuck. I'm in trouble.

I was at my old job (in fact, I was handing in my notice, and let me tell you, nothing has ever felt as good) when the delivery came. Charlie was home and signed for it. At first I think he thought I had a secret admirer or something like that, because he opened it and read the card and now he's all pissed because I didn't tell him about the job.

And because I told you.

He's never been the jealous type, but we haven't been talking much lately, partly because every time we do he makes some crack about fandom. Like, *what are you drawing*, with this knowing look that makes me feel like I'm fourteen and looking at Tiger Beat pinups. This is not good for my fangirl shame.

Ugh, I miss Con, you know? I miss being around people who get it. The fucking depth of feeling that comes from a show like this. The attachment to the characters.

And this is me, you know? *I am a fan*. It's not just something I do, it's something about the way I'm wired. It's not like this is the first time this has happened. I've always had a fandom. I've always had characters who live in my head and mess with my heart and tell me stories, and I love it.

I think Charlie thinks I don't want to get married because my heart's too wrapped up in this show.

Do you think that's true?

That's not true. I love him. I just don't know if he knows me. I don't know if I know me. Holy shit, I'm a mess right now, and the only person who fucking knows me is this eighteen year old girl on the other side of the country and I fucking miss you so much tonight, Evie, shit.

This should in no way be interpreted as your fault. I should have told Charlie about the job DAYS ago, and if I don't want to marry him I should have the decency to tell him that.

I don't know anything about anything anymore, and if you didn't read this, I wouldn't blame you.

Seriously. Thank you for the flowers. So much.

Thank you for everything.

Love.
Finn

GENA

August 11th

# Welcome to Oakmoor!

Our entire community, from the Student Welcoming Organization all the way to our top-tier professors and faculty members, looks forward to meeting you during this orientation period. Not only will this week introduce you to fellow members of your incoming class, but it will introduce you to the standards we expect here at Oakmoor, the policies of the dorm and classroom affairs, and the Oakmoor expectations for living in our vibrant community.

Through a combination of mandatory activities, small seminars, and optional (but always highly attended!) social events, our carefully organized orientation program should teach you every-thing you need to begin your journey as an integral part of the Oakmoor University community. Should you have any unan-swered questions or require any individual attention, please turn to any student wearing a Welcoming Organization T-shirt or consult with your resident advisor. And don't be afraid to ask any returning student you may see this week to help guide you as you begin your time in our community! We're all here to help.

We wish you all the best! A detailed schedule, with requirements carefully noted, is within.

—The Oakmoor University
Student Welcoming Organization

## TEXT WITH FINN

+1 815-555-9255: hey finn, ignore the weird number, it's genevieve. My phone plan expired and i'm (predictably) having a bitch of a time getting in touch with my parents for them to fix it. And of course wi-fi is out in my dorm and fuck if i know where the computer lab is. and all my roommate has is this shitty unsmart phone (it's taken me 6 minutes to type this much) so no email for gena. probably dont text me back because im already getting death looks for using her phone (is it too early to request a roommate transfer? dear lord i hope i remember to erase this text) but i wanted to let you know im here safe and thinking about u on your first day! hope you got the flowers!!

## Text with Finn

+1 401-555-0507: hey it's me again, phone hopping. still no internet and the lab isnt open until regular semester starts, OF COURSE. frustrating because no youuuu and also i need to get in touch with zack/producers about scheduling stuff. i still cant believe I agreed to do this. im such a moron.

+1 401-555-0507: you can text me back if you're here im here for a while. eli seems cool,

hes letting me hang to this for
a sec

*August 12, 11:21 AM*

+1 401-555-0507: did i tell
you im taking a drama class?
fucking ridiculous, right? But i
cant guest star next to fucking
ZACK this rusty...omg can you
imagine mal's internet glee if
i suck? ACING this class if my
life depends on it

*August 12, 11:34 AM*

+1 401-555-0507: oh you
probably cant text during work
at your new job! im so dumb.
okay im gonna give elijah back
his phone. hope everythings
okay over there, say hey to
charlie from me. everything's
pretty okay here. orientation
is fucking exhausting, running
around all the time. tired already
and classes havent even
started. sure itll be fine. love you

## TEXT WITH FINN

+1 401-555-0507: hey finny
eli said you tried to call this
number last night? he said you
sounded upset. are you there?
ive been trying to call you

*August 13, 11:16 AM*

+1 401-555-0507: im really worried babe

*August 13, 11:44 AM*

+1 401-555-0507: fuck i wish i had charlies number

*August 13, 11:56 AM*

+1 401-555-0507: fuck shit eli has to go, ill try calling from joannes phone tonight

## MEMO FROM THE FRONT OFFICE

Genevieve Goldman—

The campus pharmacy requires additional information to fill your prescriptions. Please go online to http://www.oakmoor.edu/student_services/health_center at your earliest convenience to resolve the issue.

## TEXT WITH FINN

+1 815-555-9255: u there? pick up

*August 14, 3:16 AM*

+1 815-555-9255: i'm sorry I couldnt call I was at a fucking mandatory bonfire i fucking hate fires someday ill be around when youre not either at work or its not the fucking middle of the night.

*August 14, 3:46 AM*

## LETTER TO SETH AND NAOMI
### SHOVED UNDER GENA'S MATTRESS

Hey Mom and Dad.

Orientation week is almost over. I guess really it was orientation four days but it felt like a week. Or year.

This isn't exactly what I thought it would be.

Maybe some of it is that my phone still isn't working—hopefully by the time this letter reaches you guys that will have been taken care of? I've tried calling you from the office like ten times but it says you guys are out of service, which I guess makes sense but...I'm just feeling really isolated and in all honesty fucking fuck you guys for being inaccessible.

I'd apologize but obviously I'm not going to send this because you DON'T HAVE A FUCKING ADDRESS so I don't have to.

I haven't slept in two days. Everyone's running around having this great time and making friends and oh my god let's go to the diner!! and I guess living in dorms and shit is really exciting for them or something, and everyone said I would have so much more freedom here than I did in boarding school and I'm not actually sure those people knew what freedom means. Yeah, I don't have adults breathing down my neck, but at boarding school at least they didn't run around trying to make me believe this was some sort of Disney World happiest place on earth bullshit, like everyone at this school is in on some special secret and the rest of the world has noooo idea how much fun we're having. Stoneyhall was some pretentious bullshit but at least it was honest about it.

And maybe Alanah was right. Maybe I'm part of the problem. I really did think I was some big deal for getting in here, and I guess I expected to get that slapped out of me pretty quickly, but no, everyone else is patting themselves on the back for getting in here and the upperclassmen are here now too and it's exactly the same thing. Everyone knows you got into Oakmoor. What the fuck are you BRAGGING about?

Tell me it's too early to hate this.

Tell me I'm being stupid.

Tell me I was just expecting too much.

Tell me I was an idiot for taking an acting class and thinking no one would recognize me, or thinking my fucking professor wouldn't recognize me and point me out to the entire class and then hand me a letter the second day of class telling me she can tell I have an attitude about my acting and think I'm better than everyone and I'm just here to show off and she won't indulge me.

Tell me I was an idiot to think the guy whose phone I borrowed wouldn't read my texts and sing the fucking Up Below theme song at me every time I walk by.

Tell me I was an idiot for thinking I could go to a bonfire and be totally fine with it and not have to stare at people to make sure they see the fire too and that it's real real real until someone notices and calls me creepy and then flirts with some other girl by threatening to push her in.

Tell me I was an idiot for trying to bring up my fanfic journal on someone else's phone.

Tell me I was an idiot for ever leaving my pretentious goddamn hideous easy safe Stoneyhall bubble.

Come get me and bring me to Thailand or Uzbekistan or wherever the hell you are nowadays.

-bug

### TEXT WITH JOHN C.

> +1 260-555-7175: im gonna quit school and be an actress

*August 15, 11:47 PM*

> what?

> I think you have the wrong number

*August 15, 11:53 PM*

> oh god. genevieve?

FROM: GENEVIEVE GOLDMAN <GENAZEPORAH@GMAIL.COM>
TO: FINN BARTLETT <FINN.A.BARTLETT@GMAIL.COM>
DATE: THURSDAY, AUGUST 21 5:51 PM
SUBJECT: AHHHHH

OH DEAR LORD SWEET INTERNET.

i have all these scheduling emails from producers to answer jesus christ but I will read your email and answer in JUST A SEC <3333

FROM: ZACK MARTOCCHIO <ZACKM@UPBELOW.COM>
TO: GENEVIEVE GOLDMAN <GENAZEPORAH@GMAIL.COM>
DATE: MONDAY, AUGUST 18 3:16 PM
SUBJECT: :D

Hey Gena.

I told Jack and Janet you were getting settled in to school so you probably didn't have internet right away but you were still planning to do the show and yes you'll be able to take a week off in September to come film and blah blah blah. You're welcome ;)

Hopefully if you're reading this though it means you're a step towards actually being settled in? Hope things are going well. Get in touch when you have the chance. Do you have my number?

-Z

FROM: GENEVIEVE GOLDMAN <GENAZEPORAH@GMAIL.COM>
TO: ZACK MARTOCCHIO <ZACKM@UPBELOW.COM>
DATE: THURSDAY, AUGUST 21 6:03 PM
SUBJECT: RE: :D

hey zack.

thanks so much for taking care of the grunt work. i know you're hella (as you would say--seriously, you're STILL saying that?) busy. i'll send out the proper emails now.

stuff's going really

no, fuck it, stuff's actually going really badly. i haven't been able to talk to my best friend in about a week and i'm going crazy from it and...i'm scared that going crazy might actually mean going crazy. and you're the only person i even kind of...can i still say i know you? who knows what that really means.

and i can tell from the way you played crazy-jake last season that you remember.

i don't have a phone right now so just answer this if you want to talk? or don't if i'm being too weird and we'll do a nice friendly hug when i come to set and that'll be it.

gena

FROM: GENEVIEVE GOLDMAN <GENAZEPORAH@GMAIL.COM>
TO: FINN BARTLETT <FINN.A.BARTLETT@GMAIL.COM>
DATE: THURSDAY, AUGUST 21 6:32 PM
SUBJECT: RE: CHARLIE ISSUES

holy shit i just read your email. fuck fuck fuck i am SUCH a fuck up. are you online? chatting you right now.

--g

GENA/FINN

**Genevieve:** Finn???

**Finn:** Oh my god.

**Genevieve:** oh my god shit hi

were you getting my texts did i have your number right

eli said you tried to call

**Finn:** Yeah, I felt stupid

**Genevieve:** for what??

**Finn:** I don't know. I shouldn't have called his phone. tell him I'm sorry

**Genevieve:** he's a douchebag

not gonna be telling him anything

**Finn:** uh oh, what'd he do?

**Genevieve:** it's stupid, doesn't matter

are you okay?

**Finn:** not really

**Genevieve:** tell me

**Finn:** everything's going to hell. Charlie's barely talking to me

**Genevieve:** fuck.

this is all my fault.

**Finn:** it's really not

**Genevieve:** how is it possibly not

**Finn:** because you're not the one who's been stringing him along about wanting to get married

we got into it because of the job thing, but that was just...the catalyst, you know?

if everything else had been fine that wouldn't have mattered

**Genevieve:** he thinks there's something between us, doesn't he

**Finn:** he didn't say that

exactly

**Genevieve:** fuck

**Finn:** you didn't do anything wrong

**Genevieve:** i mean, is there something between us?

there's...not not something between us.

Shit.

**Finn:** should there not be anything?

I'm allowed to fucking do...whatever this is

**Genevieve:** are you sure though

what if you're not

**Finn:** it's not like I'm married.

**Genevieve:** if it would be different if you were
then... maybe that means something

**Finn:** oh.

**Genevieve:** i mean to him

**Finn:** yeah

**Genevieve:** shit.

**Finn:** this is bullshit, I'm allowed to have a
fucking friend

**Genevieve:** i do this, don't i. i think this is a thing
that i do.

**Finn:** what?

**Genevieve:** talk people into loving me

four years of debate team and this is how i use it.
    *Sent at 7:12 PM on Thursday*

**Finn:** I'm...pretty fucking stubborn, kid

**Genevieve:** you're literally all i have

how is he not supposed to feel threatened by that

**Finn:** wait, what's going on?

**Genevieve:** what?

**Finn:** what about, um....joanie?

**Genevieve:** joanne?

**Finn:** yeah, that one

**Genevieve:** no

just no, really.

guess what her major is
    *Sent at 7:15 PM on Tuesday*

**Finn:** ummm...i have no idea. Pre-med?

**Genevieve:** theater

wish i'd known that before i started my acting class

**Finn:** yeah how's that going?

**Genevieve:** fine

**Finn:** good!

**Genevieve:** got an A- on my monologue

**Finn:** no surprise there

**Genevieve:** ha. yeah.

how's the job?

**Finn:** the job is actually great

**Genevieve:** good!

**Finn:** I have a savings account!

**Genevieve:** haha awesome
*Sent at 7:20 PM on Thursday*

**Finn:** listen, don't worry about Charlie, okay?

**Genevieve:** are you guys gonna break up?

**Finn:** I don't know

I don't want to

**Genevieve:** if you do you can come live with me in my awful dorm

**Finn:** I bet oakmoor has totally swanky dorms

**Genevieve:** one building does. they have sinks in the rooms

**Finn:** nice!

**Genevieve:** ha, not my building
*Sent at 7:26 PM on Thursday*

**Finn:** is your roommate cool?

**Genevieve:** that's joanne

**Finn:** ohhh.

**Genevieve:** yep.

**Finn:** you'll meet some people. took me a couple weeks.

**Genevieve:** her friends are always over

**Finn:** oh

**Genevieve:** they're all legacies

she's double major theater pre-law

they're all pre-somethings

they have arguments over who had the most reading this week

**Finn:** is that supposed to be a good thing?

**Genevieve:** whoever's the most miserable wins

**Finn:** fuck, my friends and I used to argue over who blew off the most reading

**Genevieve:** i've been working five hours a night since monday and it's the first week

and they have so much more work than i do and they're always here laughing and being loud and complaining and laughing while they complain

this is such stupid shit to whine about, i'm sorry.

this just isn't how i pictured it.

**Finn:** it's gonna get better

it's culture shock. it'll settle down

in a couple of weeks this is all gonna feel normal

**Genevieve:** okay

**Finn:** love you

**Genevieve:** love you

i should write another fic or something

all i'm doing is poetry
*Sent at 7:33 PM on Thursday*

**Genevieve:** now that i have internet things will be better

they all think i'm a weird loner anyway

**Finn:** yeah, but my weird loner

**Genevieve:** finn/

?

**Finn:** yeah?

**Genevieve:** are we doing something bad?
*Sent at 7:36 PM on Thursday*

**Finn:** no

**Genevieve:** okay

**Finn:** we're amazing

**Genevieve:** you make me happy

why does that have to be so fucked up.

**Finn:** other people don't get it, that's all

**Genevieve:** do you want me to talk to charlie?
*Sent at 7:39 PM on Thursday*

**Finn:** that's probably not the best idea

**Genevieve:** yeah

ugh okay i've got to go

i told this girl on my hall i'd go to the diner with her

**Finn:** good

**Genevieve:** meaning i begged her and she said okay

**Finn:** well, that's a start

**Genevieve:** yeah

start of what is the question

**Finn:** hang in there, okay?

**Genevieve:** i will. now that i have internet i can get this phone thing sorted out

i'll let you know as soon as i have service again. but i'll try to get online tonight

**Finn:** do

**Genevieve:** internet's really slow sometimes. perhaps there are more creepy weirdos in this dorm than just me

**Finn:** now all you have to do is find them!

...but don't forget me.

**Genevieve:** as if

**Finn:** go eat. love you

**Genevieve:** love you.

FINN

September 5th

Happy Labor Day, or something.

The good news is, this means it's September. The bad news is that our show doesn't come back until *October*, and this is the longest, most painful hiatus I've ever been through.

I'm getting *philosophical*, you guys. Or maybe brooding. I don't know what you'd call it.

I'm thinking a lot about Nicola, of all things.

I remember, my first time through season one, before I'd gotten involved in fandom at ALL, disliking her. And it was kind of validating to find out later that other people felt the same way and didn't want Tyler to end up with her. Some of you were downright offended by the possibility, I think, and even though that wasn't me, I kind of get it. There was something...disconcerting about that relationship.

But looking back now...why'd we all hate her so much? She wasn't a bad person. I think if I'd met her in real life, I'd have liked her okay. She was smart and dedicated and good to Ty. The time she grilled steaks on his birthday? That was actually really nice! Why'd we all get so mad about that?

I mean, I know why. It was because Ty had to miss his birthday tradition with Jake, and that was awful, and it was the first time in six years they hadn't spent their birthdays together. But Nicola wasn't a bitch for wanting to make her boyfriend dinner.

Maybe she was right in the season 1 finale.

Maybe he's too close to Jake, and it doesn't leave room for anyone else.

No fic recs today.

>>>>mmmZack reblogged this from finnblueline
>>>>Tylergirl93 reblogged this and added: Don't be a Nicola
apologist. This misses the point entirely. She WAS a bitch for
trying to change him.
    >>>>finnblueline: She wasn't trying to change him. She was
    trying to be a part of his life.
        >>>>Tylergirl93: That IS changing him. His life is his work and
        Jake.
>>>>DanniRice reblogged this and added: No fic recs? ?
    >>>>finnblueline: sorry.

### Text with Charlie

where are you?

work

early shift?

picked up a double

oh

okay.

FROM: FINN BARTLETT <FINN.A.BARTLETT@GMAIL.COM>
TO: CHARLIE THOMAS <DPS.DEALING.BOSS@GMAIL.COM>
DATE: *NONE. SAVED TO DRAFTS.*
SUBJECT: THIS SUCKS

I know you're pissed. Can we talk?

We can't keep avoiding each other. It's starting to freak me out,
being here alone with no one else I know and you drifting around
like we're strangers.

I was going to tell you about the job. It's just been so much
lately. Everything's changing, and it's really overwhelming, and...I
thought you'd be proud of me, though. I thought the fact that I
finally got a real job would matter more than...

And you put too much pressure on me. I'm twenty-two, Charlie. Is it so hard to believe that I'm not ready to talk about marriage yet? That maybe that's nothing personal?

The shit you said about Eve last night was way out of line and uncalled for. She's a good person, and she's allowed to get along well with people. If you have a problem with our friendship, your problem's with me, not with her. And anyway, I'm allowed to

## TEXT WITH CHARLIE

staying at nick's tonight, I'll see you tomorrow

*Sept 7, 5:57 pm*

okay have fun

FROM: FINN BARTLETT <FINN.A.BARTLETT@GMAIL.COM>
TO: CHARLIE THOMAS <DPS.DEALING.BOSS@GMAIL.COM>
DATE: *NONE. SAVED TO DRAFTS.*
SUBJECT: YOU SUCK

You're an asshole. Fuck off until you're ready to grow up.

FROM: FINN BARTLETT <FINN.A.BARTLETT@GMAIL.COM>
TO: JOAN BARTLETT <JOANBARTLETT4472@GMAIL.COM>
DATE: *NONE. SAVED TO DRAFTS.*
SUBJECT: RELATIONSHIPS

Things aren't going so well here. I'm starting to think I made a huge mistake. Maybe you were right. Maybe I should never have come.

How did you know when you wanted to marry Dad? Did you ever feel like you guys weren't as close as you should be, or maybe you were closer to someone else? And would he have been okay with that? These are the things they should be teaching in college. I have no idea what I'm supposed to be feeling. I can't even figure out how to sort the people in my life into categories that make sense. I feel like...shouldn't I be allowed to just love people? Why does it have to be so complicated?

I can't believe I'm saying this. I'm never going to live this down.

I think I want to come home.

FROM: FINN BARTLETT <FINN.A.BARTLETT@GMAIL.COM>
TO: JOAN BARTLETT <JOANBARTLETT4472@GMAIL.COM>
DATE: SUNDAY, SEPTEMBER 7 9:40 PM
SUBJECT: HEY

Hey

Just checking in. How's everything at home?

Work is great. Charlie and I are great. California is great.

Love you!
Finn

INTERDEPARTMENTAL MEMO
**WINDSOR PUBLISHING**

To All Employees:

Please remember that personal email is not to be checked on company time. Doing so may result in disciplinary action.

# DISCIPLINARY WRITE-UP

**Employee Name:** Stephanie Bartlett

**Manager:** Jean Parker

**Infraction:** Using company computers for personal communication; tardiness on two occasions; negative attitude

Employee was receptive to criticism and showed understanding of inappropriate actions taken. This constitutes the first written warning for Ms. Bartlett.

### TEXT WITH CHARLIE (DELETED)

I got written up at work

### TEXT WITH EVIE

you there?

uh huh good timing just got phone back. 8 billion texts to read

I just got written up at work for checking my email and...being sad on the job.

fascists

they let you text?

hiding in the bathroom...

you okay?

been better.

*Sept 9, 2:12 pm*

Charlie hasn't been home in
two days.

*Sept 9, 2:15 pm*

fuck

I need to get out of here.

🏠

GENA

# OLD TEXTS, RECEIVED AT ONCE, FOLLOWING THE REINSTATEMENT OF CELL PHONE SERVICE

## TEXT WITH FINN

Evie where are you
please don't be upset

*Aug 11, 6:15 PM*

got your weird number text,
thanks, why am I sending
you this when you won't get
it. Hey future Evie.

## TEXT WITH ALANAH

hey girl. hows college?
crestland's amazing.

levine's a good kisser
lolllllllllllll

*Aug 14, 9:17 PM*

hey come on i miss you.
we're okay right? trying
to be a grown up and shit

*Aug 15, 11:26 AM*

come visit slut best parties

*Aug 15, 10:26 PM*

## TEXT WITH DAD

sorry about no service, bug!
should be back now.

*Aug 19, 4:20 PM*

sorry, just found out that was
only our service!

fixed now, right?

*Sept 9, 5:06 PM*

## TEXT WITH +1 (416) 555-9173

is this genevieve goldman?

*Aug 16, 5:33 PM*

oh sorry this is zack

## TEXT WITH JOHN C.

i've been trying to call you

you're not even answering emails now?

*Aug 17, 10:20 AM*

that girl carolyn you texted me from was a bitch btw

probably majoring in Unhelpful

*Aug 17, 10:50 AM*

genevieve i love you

## TEXT WITH +1 (401) 555-9942

Automated Message from the Oakmoor Student Health Center. We are unable to fill your prescription without confirmation of your insurance information. Please come to the Student Health Center to resolve this issue at your earliest convenience.

## Text with Finn

on your way?

in cab now en route to airport

is this going to ruin things with charlie?

fuck charlie

*Sept 10, 1:49 PM*

is this gonna piss off your roommate?

let's hope

*Sept 10, 1:55 PM*

im a fucking homewrecker

*Sept 10, 2:23 PM*

sorry I was going through security

they didn't find my weapons of mass destruction

oh good

this feels like coming home

## Text with Zack

hey it's genevieve. you had the right number

*Sept 10, 2:41 PM*

gena!!

hey :)

actually have some downtime right now, can i call/email?

email's probably best, i'm a mess

k

FROM: ZACK MARTOCCHIO <ZACKM@UPBELOW.COM>
TO: GENEVIEVE GOLDMAN <GENAZEPORAH@GMAIL.COM>
DATE: WEDNESDAY, SEPTEMBER 10 2:56 PM
SUBJECT: :-/

Hey lady. Been thinking about you a lot, didn't know what to say.

The truth is it's been hella tough not knowing what you were up to, and maybe after nine years that's really fucking pathetic. Maybe it's that my whole damn childhood was with you or maybe it's that I looked you up a few times and couldn't ever find you (I'm not sure I would know how to use my fucking email if I didn't have a PA to tell me, thank you TV business for helping stupid people survive) but I don't think it's because of how you left so if that makes you feel any better then...let it.

That's never going to be who you were to me. You were just this sweet fucking little kid who got fucked up by the system and the stress and maybe a little by that too smart for your own good brain of yours but mostly by those chemicals like you said.

I guess what I wanted to say is you're not like a Jake, dorky little fangirl.

So don't worry.

--big brother

FROM: GENEVIEVE GOLDMAN <GENAZEPORAH@GMAIL.COM>
TO: ZACK MARTOCCHIO <ZACKM@UPBELOW.COM>
DATE: WEDNESDAY, SEPTEMBER 10 3:14 PM
SUBJECT: RE: :-/

big bro--

you're not stupid. possibly wrong (if you heard my soggy i've-just-been-crying-my-eyes-out voice you might not be so confident about not-crazy) but not stupid. so shut up. i hear you use that in interviews all the time, aww i'm just a dumb head of hair. doesn't work on me.

just like me being kind of evasive and sarcastic hasn't worked on you, huh. we can't get anything past each other.

--little sis

FROM: ZACK MARTOCCHIO <ZACKM@UPBELOW.COM>
TO: GENEVIEVE GOLDMAN <GENAZEPORAH@GMAIL.COM>
DATE: WEDNESDAY, SEPTEMBER 10 3:17 PM
SUBJECT: RE: :-/

Except that we do. Maybe we shouldn't be trying to do that.
--bb

FROM: GENEVIEVE GOLDMAN <GENAZEPORAH@GMAIL.COM>
TO: ZACK MARTOCCHIO <ZACKM@UPBELOW.COM>
DATE: WEDNESDAY, SEPTEMBER 10 3:18 PM
SUBJECT: RE: :-/

except that we do. --ls

FROM: ZACK MARTOCCHIO <ZACKM@UPBELOW.COM>
TO: GENEVIEVE GOLDMAN <GENAZEPORAH@GMAIL.COM>
DATE: WEDNESDAY, SEPTEMBER 10 3:22 PM
SUBJECT: :'(

Why were you crying?

ugh no i'm so bored of me. tell me about you. you and toby really as close as you tell people? is the girlfriend real or a publicity stunt?

keep in mind i will, of course, be selling all your answers to tabloids.

Aww, yeah, Toby's the best. Except when he's being a dick to you, obviously. (Seriously, he feels so bad. He's making you A CAKE when you come. It's gonna be awful, trust me, I know the guy.)

Miranda's real! Actually has been for way longer than people think. We dated on and off through HS and we've been solid for the past four years. She's fucking unstoppable, I'll try to make sure she's on set one of the days you're here. She hates tv so she's kind of awful but I love her. I'm attaching her with my cat on her head.

sweet lord that's adorable.

Yeah, his name's Buzz Lightyear. My nephew named him.

FROM: GENEVIEVE GOLDMAN <GENAZEPORAH@GMAIL.COM>
TO: ZACK MARTOCCHIO <ZACKM@UPBELOW.COM>
DATE: WEDNESDAY, SEPTEMBER 10 3:34 PM
SUBJECT: XD

i meant the girl!

FROM: ZACK MARTOCCHIO <ZACKM@UPBELOW.COM>
TO: GENEVIEVE GOLDMAN <GENAZEPORAH@GMAIL.COM>
DATE: WEDNESDAY, SEPTEMBER 10 3:35 PM
SUBJECT: :P

Ahhhh I see. I like the cat better.

FROM: GENEVIEVE GOLDMAN <GENAZEPORAH@GMAIL.COM>
TO: ZACK MARTOCCHIO <ZACKM@UPBELOW.COM>
DATE: WEDNESDAY, SEPTEMBER 10 3:36 PM
SUBJECT: :-,

stupid big brother.

FROM: ZACK MARTOCCHIO <ZACKM@UPBELOW.COM>
TO: GENEVIEVE GOLDMAN <GENAZEPORAH@GMAIL.COM>
DATE: WEDNESDAY, SEPTEMBER 10 3:37 PM
SUBJECT: :'(

So come on. Why were you crying?

FROM: GENEVIEVE GOLDMAN <GENAZEPORAH@GMAIL.COM>
TO: ZACK MARTOCCHIO <ZACKM@UPBELOW.COM>
DATE: WEDNESDAY, SEPTEMBER 10 3:44 PM
SUBJECT: (NO SUBJECT)

i think i'm ruining my best friend's life.

FROM: ZACK MARTOCCHIO <ZACKM@UPBELOW.COM>
TO: GENEVIEVE GOLDMAN <GENAZEPORAH@GMAIL.COM>
DATE: WEDNESDAY, SEPTEMBER 10 3:47 PM
SUBJECT: RE: (NO SUBJECT)

Boy or girl?

FROM: GENEVIEVE GOLDMAN <GENAZEPORAH@GMAIL.COM>
TO: ZACK MARTOCCHIO <ZACKM@UPBELOW.COM>
DATE: WEDNESDAY, SEPTEMBER 10 3:52 PM
SUBJECT: RE: (NO SUBJECT)

> girl. stephanie. goes by finn. she was at the con but you probably don't remember.

FROM: ZACK MARTOCCHIO <ZACKM@UPBELOW.COM>
TO: GENEVIEVE GOLDMAN <GENAZEPORAH@GMAIL.COM>
DATE: WEDNESDAY, SEPTEMBER 10 3:54 PM
SUBJECT: RE: (NO SUBJECT)

> Eesh, sorry, yeah, there was a lot of people there. Cute, though.

FROM: GENEVIEVE GOLDMAN <GENAZEPORAH@GMAIL.COM>
TO: ZACK MARTOCCHIO <ZACKM@UPBELOW.COM>
DATE: WEDNESDAY, SEPTEMBER 10 3:55 PM
SUBJECT: RE: (NO SUBJECT)

> yeah, she is.

FROM: ZACK MARTOCCHIO <ZACKM@UPBELOW.COM>
TO: GENEVIEVE GOLDMAN <GENAZEPORAH@GMAIL.COM>
DATE: WEDNESDAY, SEPTEMBER 10 3:57 PM
SUBJECT: :-)

> I meant the name...

FROM: GENEVIEVE GOLDMAN <GENAZEPORAH@GMAIL.COM>
TO: ZACK MARTOCCHIO <ZACKM@UPBELOW.COM>
DATE: WEDNESDAY, SEPTEMBER 10 4:04 PM
SUBJECT: :$ :$ :$

> fuuuuuuuck

FROM: ZACK MARTOCCHIO <ZACKM@UPBELOW.COM>
TO: GENEVIEVE GOLDMAN <GENAZEPORAH@GMAIL.COM>
DATE: WEDNESDAY, SEPTEMBER 10 4:08 PM
SUBJECT: :D

> Still crushing on girls, curious little eight year old?

FROM: GENEVIEVE GOLDMAN <GENAZEPORAH@GMAIL.COM>
TO: ZACK MARTOCCHIO <ZACKM@UPBELOW.COM>
DATE: WEDNESDAY, SEPTEMBER 10 4:11 PM
SUBJECT: :(

> is that relevant?

FROM: ZACK MARTOCCHIO <ZACKM@UPBELOW.COM>
TO: GENEVIEVE GOLDMAN <GENAZEPORAH@GMAIL.COM>
DATE: WEDNESDAY, SEPTEMBER 10 4:12 PM
SUBJECT: :P

> You tell me.

FROM: GENEVIEVE GOLDMAN <GENAZEPORAH@GMAIL.COM>
TO: ZACK MARTOCCHIO <ZACKM@UPBELOW.COM>
DATE: WEDNESDAY, SEPTEMBER 10 4:38 PM
SUBJECT: (NO SUBJECT)

> she's married. practically. okay not practically. but her boyfriend
> wants to marry her and deep down she wants to marry him
> and she doesn't know but i do, except the husband has (WE
> HAVEN'T) set this up as a genevieve vs charlie kind of situation
> and right now she's on her way to me so like...god, fuck me. i
> don't know why my tendency for pushing everyone away the
> second after i let them in doesn't apply to her. she's immune to
> me like you are i guess.
>
> and maybe that's the issue, that you both have this weird thing
> where you know too many parts of me. i mean we didn't talk in
> years and you still know me better than my ex-boyfriend who
> thinks he loves me because i'm good in bed and i held his hand
> when his mom was dying and i let him read my weird feminist
> poetry from my high school phase back when i hated everyone
> and not just me. and him.
>
> but you know weird child actor me and crazy me and now you
> know eighteen year old rambly me and you're not judging me for
> coming to a con for your show like a stalker person or for running
> out of there or for, let's hope, having crushes on girls. ex-boy

didn't get all of that. ex-bff didn't get all of that. because why would i tell people? why is telling someone everything something people need? i didn't have you for years and as nice as it is talking now, and as much as i all the time thought about getting in touch with you, it wasn't because i needed you to fill some void in my life and i'm pretty sure you feel the same way so whatever.

and then Finn comes along.

this fucking girl, she has no damn idea how amazing she is, and i think if she did then maybe she'd understand why charlie loves her enough to marry her and there we go to the part where i'm ruining my best friend's life, because instead of telling her she's amazing i'm letting her come stay with me, and instead of telling her she needs to forget me and let him love her i'm letting her come stay with me, and instead of feeling bad about those things i'm here crying because i know that at some point she's going to have to leave and go back home and i don't want her to

she knows everything about me. she knows about man of the house. she knows about me coming to your show. she knows about my parents never being home and the issues i'm having right now at college and weird shit i'm into in bed and what i want to do when i grow up and how i went crazy and how i hear fire alarms in my sleep and how i think i might be going crazy again and what if i tell her too much and finally push her away, and why haven't i figured out how to do that yet.

i'm crying because my practically-married friend can't live with me in my dorm forever.

so there you go.

FROM: ZACK MARTOCCHIO <ZACKM@UPBELOW.COM>
TO: GENEVIEVE GOLDMAN <GENAZEPORAH@GMAIL.COM>
DATE: WEDNESDAY, SEPTEMBER 10 4:49 PM
SUBJECT: RE: (NO SUBJECT)

College is bad?

--bb

FROM: GENEVIEVE GOLDMAN <GENAZEPORAH@GMAIL.COM>
TO: ZACK MARTOCCHIO <ZACKM@UPBELOW.COM>
DATE: WEDNESDAY, SEPTEMBER 10 4:53 PM
SUBJECT: RE: (NO SUBJECT)

i have to go, she'll be here soon.

## TEXT WITH JOHN C.

you don't love me

wtf? THAT'S what you have to say? i've been fucking FREAKING OUT.

why

because going back to acting is your version of suicide.

suicide is my version of suicide

is that supposed to be a joke?

stop telling me you love me.

fine.

you don't even know me

what the hell?

you know me knowing you.

### Important Things

I've grown pretty sure
that I am two-thirds cliché.
One-third girl. Or you.

### Pretty Things

I sat still. You tore
us to pieces. I pictured
sweet photos of me.

### Real Things

But, dear, the truth is
no one wants to hear these things.
Even me. Sorry.

FINN

Is it normal to have younger friends?    🔍

FROM SOCIALGRACE.NET

**KevinAce writes:** "Is it normal to have friends who are four or five years younger than me?"

**Foodie writes:** "My best friend is five years younger. I don't think it's that strange."

**BaseballFan writes:** "It is when you're kids, but as you get older age matters less and less. You can be 35 and have a friend who's 30, and that isn't weird at all."

**Admin writes:** "Age doesn't matter, but if your feelings go beyond friendship you should tread carefully until both parties involved are of age. -- Grace"

How big is Rhode Island?    🔍

FROM WIKIPEDIA, THE FREE ENCYCLOPEDIA

Rhode Island's official nickname is "The Ocean State," a reference to the state's geography, since Rhode Island has several large bays and inlets that amount to about 14% of its total area. Its land area is 1,045 square miles (2,710 km$^2$), but its total area is significantly larger.

Oakmoor University    🔍

FROM OAKMOOR.EDU

Oakmoor students make up a vibrant community with a zest for life. Both in and out of the classroom, young men and women of Oakmoor are curious and involved citizens of the world. Ours is a close-knit community that offers a unique camaraderie. Indeed, the bonds formed here are truly life-long friendships.

Our faculty and staff are deeply committed to the well-being of each of our students and to providing a support network that will enable you to make Oakmoor your home.

| How do you know when you're in love? | 🔍 |

FROM HEALTHANDWELLNESS.COM

## Top Signs You're in Love

- You find yourself thinking about your crush all the time, even when you're apart.

- Work, family, and other interests suddenly take a backseat to the object of your affection.

- You're constantly on the alert for incoming calls, texts, or emails.

- Though your loved one may have faults, you see them as merely endearing quirks.

- You feel as though you could talk to your partner forever and never run out of things to say.

- Empathy. You hurt at the thought of your love in pain.

| Up Below season 4 spoiler | 🔍 |

FROM SPOILERNEWS.COM

## Season 4 – Evanson's Betrayal, Jake's Behavior, And A Mystery Guest?

Posted by Alison K

September 9

As we're all aware by now, Ben Evanson is not who he says he is. The question is, who is he?

It looks like this question, at least, will finally be answered in the upcoming season of *Up Below*. Carl Casden has confirmed that he will be returning for at least seven episodes next fall, so we can look forward to a continuation of the Evanson arc and hopefully a more thorough examination of our favorite shady character.

Meanwhile, a recurring theme throughout season 3 has been Jake behaving in untrustworthy ways. Likely there's something up his sleeve – perhaps a semi-permanent split from Tyler? Longtime fans of the show should be excited at the prospect of the leads getting some time apart and having the opportunity to develop as characters independent of each other!

The producers hint at an exciting guest star in an early episode of season 4.

Could this be someone we've seen before – perhaps Katherine Miller (Nicola) returning as a love interest for Tyler?

*This post has received 453 negative votes.*

---

| Mad World _EvenIf | Q |
|---|---|

AN EXCERPT FROM _EVENIF'S JOURNAL ENTRY "MAD WORLD," FEBRUARY 6TH

The problem, he begins to figure out, is that everything is too fast except for the colors. While everything else races by, repeating, a flip-book coaxed one way and the other, back and forth, the same black and white people walking across a sketched street again and again, the colors drag and stall and mush together. Purple and orange combined do not make a color. Green and red. Mustard and magenta.

But today they do.

"I don't have names for the colors," he says, because he doesn't know how to write it down. "Why won't someone tell me the names?"

*Train* says a voice in his ear. *Turkeyball. Superman. These aren't colors.*

*Whatever you want, Jacob.*

A few hours later fire starts grabbing him from both sides of his head. It snakes down his throat until it swells shut and kisses his cheeks with flames and whispers in his ear the colors of crab grass and the insides of seashells.

It's so hot, he is a melting popsicle, he is back and forth melting and drowning in himself, flipping back and forth, and it will never stop. He will sit on this floor and fire will shake him like a snow globe for the rest of his life.

He wants that to be a very short time.

Arms appear behind him, slide under his, pull him back against a chest.

*I'll name whatever you want, Jake,* the voice says, the rough hands against his t-shirt say. He feels the pressure of a chin on top of his head and knows, *Tyler Tyler Tyler.* He knows a word.

"I'll give you whatever you want," Tyler says. "Just stay."

GENA/FINN

**Finn:** ...is she always like this? or is this for my benefit?

**Genevieve:** ha, like which part

joanne is not known for doing anything for other people's benefit, unless it benefits them to hear techno for 6 hours straight

**Finn:** she doesn't shut up!

my god, I mean, I've seen some terrible roommates, but....

**Genevieve:** you're lucky natalie's not here

you want to talk about not shutting up

**Finn:** who the hell is Natalie?

**Genevieve:** her best friend forever!!!!!!!!!

**Finn:** oh boy I must have missed the PSA!

**Genevieve:** did you miss the glowing note she left on her whiteboard

YOU CRAZY SLUT I LOVE YOUUUUU

now i know why everyone hated alanah

**Finn:** a lot of people love crazy sluts

**Genevieve:** i must hope so

**Finn:** hush

**Genevieve:** want to borrow my headphones?

**Finn:** no, cause you need those

**Genevieve:** i wonder if she knows we're messaging each other

**Finn:** I wonder if she knows we're talking ABOUT HER

**Genevieve:** you know she didn't even CARE when we didn't have internet?

**Finn:** ...that's kind of abnormal

**Genevieve:** some kind of sorcery

**Finn:** I bet she plays intramural sports, doesn't she

**Genevieve:** crew

**Finn:** the boat thing?

**Genevieve:** yup

**Finn:** people still DO that?

**Genevieve:** she tried to get me to join and be cockswain or whatever

cockswains have to be little

that's my only value here so far

hey gena, you're short

**Finn:** hahahahaha

COCKSWAIN

**Genevieve:** you're twelve

**Finn:** oh jesus she's staring at me

**Genevieve:** NO SUDDEN MOVEMENTS

**Finn:** what's for dinner around here?

**Genevieve:** you can check the diner menu online

**Finn:** okay

hey, boeuf bourguignon

**Genevieve:** sounds about right

**Finn:** I have no idea what that is

want to go check it out?

**Genevieve:** i can't

**Finn:** why?

**Genevieve:** i have four psych chapters to read

and i'm not even done with this write up

**Finn:** you've been studying for three hours kid, you can take a break

**Genevieve:** it doesn't work that way

they don't care how long it takes me
   *Sent at 5:50 PM on Thursday*

**Finn:** are you crying?

**Genevieve:** i don't know

**Finn:** oh kid...

you're taking a break. let's go take a walk or something. look at the city

**Genevieve:** everyone else here is FINE, they go out every night and they come back all loud and they're acing everything, how the fuck did i even get in here someone must have thought i was still famous or some shit.

fuck, i'm sorry, i'm being an awful host

let me find you the train schedule and you can go to the art school and look at their galleries

**Finn:** no, hey, that's not what I meant

I'm staying with you

**Genevieve:** consider what you're saying

you just said you're staying with JOANNE

**Finn:** fuck Joanne

**Genevieve:** are you prepared to make that sacrifice

**Finn:** yes

**Genevieve:** i'm sorry. i'll take you somewhere tomorrow i promise

maybe i should skip all my classes

**Finn:** I had no idea it was this bad

**Genevieve:** yeah i'm gonna skip everything tomorrow.

Okay.

**Finn:** that's what you want?

**Genevieve:** i don't know

i can't go

i'm not ready

**Finn:** don't do it because of me. I think you could use the break, personally, but you don't have to entertain me

we'll just stay here and relax and Joanne won't be here and you can talk it all out

**Genevieve:** okay, but i have to do my psych280 paper too

but i can do that while we talk. Yeah.

**Finn:** Evie, god, don't cry...

**Genevieve:** i'm sorry i'll stop

god, i wish she'd leave.

oh look, here's natalie

**Finn:** cuddle me. maybe we can scare 'em off

**Genevieve:** coming

FINN

Hi.

I really fucked up.

I'm so sorry. I don't know what to say. I don't even know where to start.

I'm sorry I came to Providence when things were bad between us instead of staying to try and fix it.

I'm sorry I let myself get attached to someone else. You were right, it's not simple, we're not just friends and I feel horrible and I never ever fucking wanted to do that to you. I promise nothing happened between us, I don't even know if it's like that, but it's big and intense and all these feelings, I'm in love with this fucking girl, holy shit, Charlie, I love you so much and I'm so sorry.

I'm sorry for not making you the center of my life every damn day.

I'm sorry for moving to California without knowing whether I was taking you seriously or not, because you deserve better and I should know after three years and I do take you seriously. I don't know what I'm hiding from. I don't know what I'm waiting for.

Please, please, please tell me you got this.

Please tell me you don't hate me.

Please tell me I haven't ruined everything.
I love you.
-me

Are you still with her?

Yeah. She's sleeping. I can't.

I keep thinking of this time on *Up Below* when Jake was

Yeah. She's sleeping. I can't.

I keep thinking of junior year, when you decided to move to California and we didn't know if we were going to make it. I was so scared you'd meet someone else and fall in love and forget all about me. And you never did. You called every night, and you visited, and you were there for me all through senior year when classes were insane and I didn't have anybody. You were the best friend I could have asked for.

You've always been the best everything I could ask for.

I hate myself for coming out here. I feel so sick. All I can say in my defense is that I love you too. I've never forgotten that. I may be scared of the future, I may be pathetic and distant and unable to give you what you need, but I have never not loved you.

FROM: CHARLIE THOMAS <DPS.DEALING.BOSS@GMAIL.COM>
TO: FINN BARTLETT <FINN.A.BARTLETT@GMAIL.COM>
DATE: FRIDAY, SEPTEMBER 12 11:32 PM
SUBJECT: RE: I'M SORRY

I don't hate you.

FROM: FINN BARTLETT <FINN.A.BARTLETT@GMAIL.COM>
TO: CHARLIE THOMAS <DPS.DEALING.BOSS@GMAIL.COM>
DATE: SATURDAY, SEPTEMBER 13 2:33 AM
SUBJECT: RE: I'M SORRY

Yeah??

FROM: CHARLIE THOMAS <DPS.DEALING.BOSS@GMAIL.COM>
TO: FINN BARTLETT <FINN.A.BARTLETT@GMAIL.COM>
DATE: FRIDAY, SEPTEMBER 12 11:35 PM
SUBJECT: RE: I'M SORRY

I love you.

FROM: FINN BARTLETT <FINN.A.BARTLETT@GMAIL.COM>
TO: CHARLIE THOMAS <DPS.DEALING.BOSS@GMAIL.COM>
DATE: SATURDAY, SEPTEMBER 13 2:36 AM
SUBJECT: RE: I'M SORRY

Oh my god, baby, I love you too.

FROM: CHARLIE THOMAS <DPS.DEALING.BOSS@GMAIL.COM>
TO: FINN BARTLETT <FINN.A.BARTLETT@GMAIL.COM>
DATE: FRIDAY, SEPTEMBER 12 11:39 PM
SUBJECT: RE: I'M SORRY

You just took off. I had to find out from a fucking text message.
Did you even tell them at your work?

FROM: FINN BARTLETT <FINN.A.BARTLETT@GMAIL.COM>
TO: CHARLIE THOMAS <DPS.DEALING.BOSS@GMAIL.COM>
DATE: SATURDAY, SEPTEMBER 13 2:45 AM
SUBJECT: RE: I'M SORRY

I've been burning sick days. It's really fucking terrifying, actually.
I'm calling them every morning faking sick and hoping they don't

tell me I need to get my ass back into the office or I'm fired.

...This is really irresponsible. I don't know what's wrong with me. Things have been so nuts lately. Shit, I hope they're not mad. I hope you're not mad. I can't even look at myself. I can't even believe I'm this person. I have EVERYTHING anybody could want and I'm being SO SELFISH. How do you not hate me?

I'm ruining everything.

Tell me how to make this right.

FROM: CHARLIE THOMAS <DPS.DEALING.BOSS@GMAIL.COM>
TO: FINN BARTLETT <FINN.A.BARTLETT@GMAIL.COM>
DATE: FRIDAY, SEPTEMBER 12 11:51 PM
SUBJECT: RE: I'M SORRY

You know how.

I'm not proud of myself for this, and the last thing I want is to keep you from making friends, but you said yourself that this wasn't just friendship. Ever since you went to Chicago, she's all you talk about. You're blowing off work. You're walking out on me. I don't know what happened there, and I don't know what's happening between you now, but whatever it is, it isn't "nothing."

I'm really not accusing you of anything but what you already admitted. You're too attached. There's no room for me when you're that tied to someone else. So I'm sorry, and I never wanted to put you in this situation, but you have to make a choice.

Come home. Come home to work and to me and don't go back. Let me be your best friend, the way we were back in Iowa. If you can do that, we'll be all right.

FROM: FINN BARTLETT <FINN.A.BARTLETT@GMAIL.COM>
TO: CHARLIE THOMAS <DPS.DEALING.BOSS@GMAIL.COM>
DATE: SATURDAY, SEPTEMBER 13 2:56 AM
SUBJECT: RE: I'M SORRY

Are you saying I can't talk to her anymore?

She's lonely. She's my friend and she's alone and having a hell of
a time adjusting to college. I can't just cut her loose.

God, she's sleeping and she has no idea. This is really going to
wreck her, I'm her only friend and she'll think I don't want her...

FROM: CHARLIE THOMAS <DPS.DEALING.BOSS@GMAIL.COM>
TO: FINN BARTLETT <FINN.A.BARTLETT@GMAIL.COM>
DATE: SATURDAY, SEPTEMBER 13 12:03 AM
SUBJECT: RE: I'M SORRY

I can't tell you who you can and can't talk to, Finn. I'm not that
guy. But I need you to keep your distance emotionally. You decide
if you can do that and still be friends.

And, I mean, you can choose her over me if that's really where
you are. I didn't ask you to make a choice without knowing I might
not be it. I just need you to be honest with me about where I
stand. I love you, and I don't want to keep doing that if I'm always
going to come second.

God, I can't believe this is happening.

I hope you come home. I really miss you, Finn, I miss us.

FROM: FINN BARTLETT <FINN.A.BARTLETT@GMAIL.COM>
TO: CHARLIE THOMAS <DPS.DEALING.BOSS@GMAIL.COM>
DATE: *NONE. SAVED TO DRAFTS.*
SUBJECT: RE: I'M SORRY

I can't. I love her. She needs me. Don't make me choose. I don't
want to

FROM: FINN BARTLETT <FINN.A.BARTLETT@GMAIL.COM>
TO: CHARLIE THOMAS <DPS.DEALING.BOSS@GMAIL.COM>
DATE: *NONE. SAVED TO DRAFTS.*
SUBJECT: RE: I'M SORRY

> You're being really unreasonable. There's nothing wrong with me
> having a

FROM: FINN BARTLETT <FINN.A.BARTLETT@GMAIL.COM>
TO: CHARLIE THOMAS <DPS.DEALING.BOSS@GMAIL.COM>
DATE: SATURDAY, SEPTEMBER 13 3:27 AM
SUBJECT: RE: I'M SORRY

> I miss us too.
> I'll be on a plane in the morning.

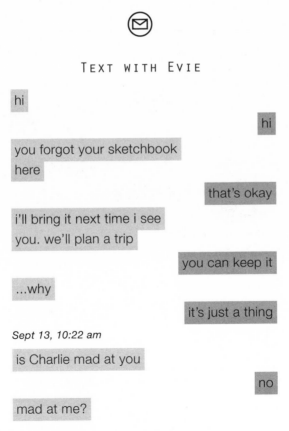

## TEXT WITH EVIE

hi

hi

you forgot your sketchbook here

that's okay

i'll bring it next time i see you. we'll plan a trip

you can keep it

...why

it's just a thing

*Sept 13, 10:22 am*

is Charlie mad at you

no

mad at me?

he's not mad

*Sept 13, 10:25 pm*

i meant you

no, evie

we're not planning another
trip, huh

*Sept 13, 10:26 pm*

can you say something

*Sept 13, 10:31 pm*

I can't not love you too much

i'm sorry

i'm sorry

*Sept 13, 10:36 pm*

i can do better. don't go

you didn't do anything wrong.
It's my fault

*Sept 13, 10:41 pm*

my plane's boarding

will you text me when you
land?

*Sept 13, 10:45 pm*

Finn?

GENA

I watch a lot of *Up Below* and write a lot of fanfic and shoot a lot of heroin. One of those is false. I do a mean French braid.

## SEP 18 — Hiatus Schmiatus

We are a mere TWO WEEKS AWAY from the premiere!! Glory and hallelujah to all above and of course ESPECIALLY below. I don't know about you guys, but I definitely don't think I could go a SINGLE EXTRA BLESSED DAY without my Jake and Tyler fix. My life is so empty of unconditional support and unspoken love! Where are the small bickering matches the show tries to turn into big dramas? Where are the plot holes that will never be filled in? Where is the case of the week no one cares about? MY LIFE NEEDS THESE LITTLE THINGS, INTERNET.

No but seriously I could not possibly be more excited about the show coming back. I'd say it's the thing in my life I'm excited about more than anything...EXCEPT OH YEAH THERE'S ONE OTHER THING.

I'm going to be in episode six!!!!! I leave for filming in three days!

Before you call me a liar and a skank and whatnot, there are a few things you should know:

--I'm just a cameo. I'm not in the plot. I'm not going to be a returning character. I don't make out with anyone.

--it's total pure nepotism, so go RAGE AGAINST THE SYSTEM.

So obviously this is me being a little more forthright about the Girl Behind the Curtain than I usually am, but I decided I'd probably fucking die if I tried to keep this to myself any longer and YOU ARE MY BESTEST FRIENDS, INTERNET. So there you go. Pathetic and lonely, yes. But pathetic and lonely and UNDOCUMENTED ON NETWORK TV?

Not on your life.

## 12 Comments

Leave a comment

**Bluebloody**
oh my god what??? this is AMAZING tell us EVERYTHING

> **_EvenIf**
> heehee all in good time

**MioMy**
so does this mean you've read a script? DOES THIS MEAN YOU KNOW SPOILERS

> **_EvenIf**
> I am not at liberty to say, but trust me that it's gonna be a goooood season...

> > **MioMy**
> > oh god you tease why do I like you

**Tylergirl93**
so you slept with him, right?

> **_EvenIf**
> ?

> > **Tylergirl93**
> > you slept with zack, thats how come.

> > > **_EvenIf**
> > > lol

**SwingLowMySweet**
god, this is so cool. There better be pics!

> **_EvenIf**
> of COURSE!

FROM: ELEANOR MARRIOT <E.MARRIOT@OAKMOOR.EDU>
TO: GENEVIEVE GOLDMAN <G.GOLDMAN@OAKMOOR.EDU>
DATE: FRIDAY, SEPTEMBER 19 4:16 PM
SUBJECT: ATTENDANCE

Genevieve—

You've now missed four discussion sections out of a total of twelve for the semester. Please see me to discuss if there might be a way for you to make up the work somehow and be able to pass this course. Landleman's strict. This is going to take a lot of work.

Best,
Eleanor Marriot
Teacher's Assistant for Dr. Patricia Landleman, HIST314G

FROM: STUDENT HEALTH CENTER
<HEALTHANDWELLNESS@OAKMOOR.EDU>
TO: GENEVIEVE GOLDMAN <G.GOLDMAN@OAKMOOR.EDU>
DATE: FRIDAY, SEPTEMBER 19 4:42 PM
SUBJECT: MISSED APPOINTMENT

Genevieve Goldman:

This notice serves to alert you that you missed your appointment at the Health Center scheduled for September 13. As this appointment was not cancelled with 24 hours' notice, your student account has been charged for the full amount.

TEXT WITH ALANAH

hey gurrrrl

*Sept 19, 10:21 PM*

hey!!

still having fun?

fuck yeah, college forever. you?

best years of our life

preach. when are you visiting?

whenever, my profs dont care about attendance

next week??

okay

awesome bring ritalin

k

🏠

FROM: GENEVIEVE GOLDMAN <GENAZEPORAH@GMAIL.COM>
TO: FINN BARTLETT <FINN.A.BARTLETT@GMAIL.COM>
DATE: SATURDAY, SEPTEMBER 20 7:02 PM
SUBJECT: MISSED CALL?

hey there! i had a missed call from you, did i get pocket dialed?

anyway i thought you might want to see some pictures from set! check 'em out...doesn't zack look gorgeous?

having a great time here. they're trying to talk me into coming back for a future episode or two and i have to say, i'm considering it! it's just been so much fun. hope everything's cool with you! tell charlie i say hey!

--genevieve

✉

GENA/FINN

FROM: FINN BARTLETT <FINN.A.BARTLETT@GMAIL.COM>
TO: GENEVIEVE GOLDMAN <GENAZEPORAH@GMAIL.COM>
DATE: SATURDAY, SEPTEMBER 20 6:15 PM
SUBJECT: RE: MISSED CALL?

Hey.

Not a pocket dial. It wasn't anything important, though.

Thanks for the pics. Glad you're having fun. Are things better on the school front?

Everything's fine here. Still at my job, thank god. Charlie's good.

FROM: GENEVIEVE GOLDMAN <GENAZEPORAH@GMAIL.COM>
TO: FINN BARTLETT <FINN.A.BARTLETT@GMAIL.COM>
DATE: SATURDAY, SEPTEMBER 20 9:34 PM
SUBJECT: RE: MISSED CALL?

school's okay. i might be dropping out.

work's okay?

FROM: FINN BARTLETT <FINN.A.BARTLETT@GMAIL.COM>
TO: GENEVIEVE GOLDMAN <GENAZEPORAH@GMAIL.COM>
DATE: SATURDAY, SEPTEMBER 20 6:47 PM
SUBJECT: RE: MISSED CALL?

Dropping out?? Why? Are you sure you're okay?

FROM: GENEVIEVE GOLDMAN <GENAZEPORAH@GMAIL.COM>
TO: FINN BARTLETT <FINN.A.BARTLETT@GMAIL.COM>
DATE: SATURDAY, SEPTEMBER 20 9:55 PM
SUBJECT: RE: MISSED CALL?

i got a shitty grade on my scene performance in my acting class and then i come here on set and they tell me i'm doing a great job and i believe them. so why would i go back?

FROM: FINN BARTLETT <FINN.A.BARTLETT@GMAIL.COM>
TO: GENEVIEVE GOLDMAN <GENAZEPORAH@GMAIL.COM>
DATE: SATURDAY, SEPTEMBER 20 7:02 PM
SUBJECT: RE: MISSED CALL?

> So don't quit school, quit acting class.

FROM: GENEVIEVE GOLDMAN <GENAZEPORAH@GMAIL.COM>
TO: FINN BARTLETT <FINN.A.BARTLETT@GMAIL.COM>
DATE: SATURDAY, SEPTEMBER 20 10:14 PM
SUBJECT: RE: MISSED CALL?

> too late in the semester to drop a class.

FROM: FINN BARTLETT <FINN.A.BARTLETT@GMAIL.COM>
TO: GENEVIEVE GOLDMAN <GENAZEPORAH@GMAIL.COM>
DATE: SATURDAY, SEPTEMBER 20 7:16 PM
SUBJECT: RE: MISSED CALL?

> You know, there are resources on campus to help you out if you're
> unhappy. Is Joanne still giving you hell?

FROM: GENEVIEVE GOLDMAN <GENAZEPORAH@GMAIL.COM>
TO: FINN BARTLETT <FINN.A.BARTLETT@GMAIL.COM>
DATE: SATURDAY, SEPTEMBER 20 10:20 PM
SUBJECT: RE: MISSED CALL?

> she has a boyfriend, she's never around.

FROM: FINN BARTLETT <FINN.A.BARTLETT@GMAIL.COM>
TO: GENEVIEVE GOLDMAN <GENAZEPORAH@GMAIL.COM>
DATE: SATURDAY, SEPTEMBER 20 7:31 PM
SUBJECT: RE: MISSED CALL?

> Okay...can we talk? Your first email seemed really happy, and your
> journals have been so upbeat lately, but now you're talking about
> dropping out of school and it's making me worry.
>
> Are you okay, really?
>
> Because the truth is, I'm kind of not.

Charlie and I are doing great, and he's fucking everything I need him to be, and he watches Up Below reruns with me and asks about my art in a nice, not judgmental way (not that I'm drawing lately), and I'm even thinking getting married someday might not be so bad.

But I just miss you. I just fucking do.

Just tell me you're okay? I'm worried, kid.

FROM: GENEVIEVE GOLDMAN <GENAZEPORAH@GMAIL.COM>
TO: FINN BARTLETT <FINN.A.BARTLETT@GMAIL.COM>
DATE: SATURDAY, SEPTEMBER 20 10:37 PM
SUBJECT: STOP

don't do this.

FROM: FINN BARTLETT <FINN.A.BARTLETT@GMAIL.COM>
TO: GENEVIEVE GOLDMAN <GENAZEPORAH@GMAIL.COM>
DATE: SATURDAY, SEPTEMBER 20 7:40 PM
SUBJECT: RE: STOP

I've been TRYING not to do this.
Just tell me you're okay and I'll leave you alone.

FROM: GENEVIEVE GOLDMAN <GENAZEPORAH@GMAIL.COM>
TO: FINN BARTLETT <FINN.A.BARTLETT@GMAIL.COM>
DATE: SATURDAY, SEPTEMBER 20 10:43 PM
SUBJECT: RE: STOP

don't ask me that. don't act like I can tell you.

FROM: FINN BARTLETT <FINN.A.BARTLETT@GMAIL.COM>
TO: GENEVIEVE GOLDMAN <GENAZEPORAH@GMAIL.COM>
DATE: SATURDAY, SEPTEMBER 20 7:44 PM
SUBJECT: RE: STOP

I still care, you know.

FROM: GENEVIEVE GOLDMAN <GENAZEPORAH@GMAIL.COM>
TO: FINN BARTLETT <FINN.A.BARTLETT@GMAIL.COM>
DATE: SATURDAY, SEPTEMBER 20 10:45 PM
SUBJECT: RE: STOP

> yeah.

FROM: FINN BARTLETT <FINN.A.BARTLETT@GMAIL.COM>
TO: GENEVIEVE GOLDMAN <GENAZEPORAH@GMAIL.COM>
DATE: SATURDAY, SEPTEMBER 20 7:49 PM
SUBJECT: RE: STOP

> Damn it, Evie.

FROM: GENEVIEVE GOLDMAN <GENAZEPORAH@GMAIL.COM>
TO: FINN BARTLETT <FINN.A.BARTLETT@GMAIL.COM>
DATE: SATURDAY, SEPTEMBER 20 10:53 PM
SUBJECT: RE: STOP

> that's not my name.

FROM: FINN BARTLETT <FINN.A.BARTLETT@GMAIL.COM>
TO: GENEVIEVE GOLDMAN <GENAZEPORAH@GMAIL.COM>
DATE: SATURDAY, SEPTEMBER 20 8:25 PM
SUBJECT: RE: STOP

> Okay, you know what? This wasn't what I wanted. I never fucking
> wanted this. I was doing fucking fine. And you had to go and be
> all wonderful and weird and make me love you when you KNEW I
> had a boyfriend, and instead of putting a goddamn label on things
> so I could point to us and say we're fucking FRIENDS, you made
> sure I knew how COMPLICATED it all was so I couldn't explain it
> away. You left me no fucking WAY to be around you without my
> boyfriend feeling threatened, and now I have to prioritize him and
> you just don't want to know me anymore. Fine.
>
> I just hope you know that I fall asleep worried about you and I
> wake up worried about you and there's not a fucking thing I can
> do about it and my life is a mess and I don't think I can ever stop
> loving you.

you know what would be nice?

if people would stop equating worrying about me with loving me.

you're worried about me. awesome. john's worried about me. everyone's SO CONCERNED, gena. but you know what happens when people are WORRIED? they decide you're too much fucking work, or too, i don't know, COMPLICATED, and you're always going to be the thing that ruined their fucking life, and they resent you for existing and then they resent you for trying to leave, so maybe i'm being normal and bubbly and like i'm supposed to be and maybe there's a chance that people will go back to living their lives and leave me alone and stop making me their excuse for being miserable and needing to go and then blaming me for LETTING them go. i'm just the chick you're supposed to text when you're drunk and that's IT, i didn't ask to be anyone's weird and wonderful or anyone's fucking REASON.

i'm fucking fine, okay? so you can have your life and your boyfriend get married and have babies and i'll be all right. okay?

Okay, Gena. I'll leave you alone. I'm glad you're fine.

FINN

## Explosion on Set of TV Show Kills 3, Injures 5

September 28
6:21 pm

A fire and subsequent explosion on the set of the popular TV series *Up Below* resulted in three fatalities this afternoon.

The incident was caused by a malfunctioning lighting device, sources say. Filming was taking place in an unfamiliar location in a studio the network had never previously used.

Five people suffered burns, lacerations, and complications from smoke inhalation and were taken to an undisclosed hospital in Toronto. The identities and conditions of the injured are not known at this time.

The Royal Canadian Mounted Police are investigating, but are unable to release any details of their investigation.

"At this stage, we do not suspect deliberate sabotage," says RCMP Chief Richard Whelan. "It appears to have been an unfortunate accident caused by a delayed response to a dangerous technical malfunction. Our hope is to keep this investigation short and put the matter to rest quickly."

*Up Below*, a crime drama starring Zachary Martocchio and Tobias Frost, was scheduled to begin its fourth season in just a few days. It is unknown whether the season premiere will be airing on schedule.

Out of respect for the families, the names of the deceased are not being released at this time.

$\otimes$

just heard there was an explosion. tell me you're okay.

*Sept 28, 6:23 pm*

it's fine if you're mad but just tell me you're all right. Please.

## TEXT WITH CHARLIE

holy shit, there was an explosion on the set of UB

everyone okay??

it says 3 people died...

god.

*Sept 28, 6:25 pm*

isn't evie shooting with them this week?

I mean maybe she knows more details

texted her but no answer

how long ago?

couple minutes

I'm sure she'll get back to you as soon as she can

love you

need me to come home?

you have to work. I'm fine.

## TEXT WITH EVIE

hey, haven't heard from you,

checking in again. I'm scared. please text

*Sept 28, 7:01 pm*

are you okay?

*Sept 28, 7:06 pm*

gena?

⌂

# *finnblueline*

////////////////////////////////////////////////////////////////

September 28th
//////////////////

Has anyone seen this article?

I'm assuming this is real?

Does anybody know anything?

>>>>DanniRice reblogged this and added: Oh...my god. I hadn't seen it. Fatalities?!

>>>>finnblueline says: this is really scary

>>>>Tylergirl93 reblogged this and added: Everyone: _EvenIf was on set this week. Is anyone in touch with her?

>>>>MioMy says: oh my god

>>>>SwingLowMySweet says: she hasn't posted in a while and she promised pics.

>>>>Tylergirl93 says: oh that's not a good sign

>>>>finnblueline says: this just happened a few hours ago

>>>>Tylergirl93 says: you're friends with her, right?

>>>>finnblueline says: I haven't heard anything

>>>>mmmZack reblogged this and added: does ANYONE know if the guys are okay? And what does this mean for the season premiere? I will DIE if it gets delayed.

>>>>slotohes says: this is the most insensitive thing I've ever heard. People are actually dead, asshole. Of course the TV show is going to get delayed. You're not the center of the fucking universe.

>>>>MioMy reblogged this and added: AMEN.

>>>>DanniRice reblogged this

>>>>mmmZack says: I meant it figuratively but if you have no sense of irony that's your problem I guess

>>>>slotohes says: that's not even what irony is.

>>>>popstotheweasel reblogged this and added: this picture leaked from the set after the explosion. It's pretty low quality. You can see Carl Casden pretty clearly, but I can't tell who any of the other people are. take a look.

>>>>Tylergirl93 says: any news of Toby?

>>>>popstotheweasel says: I don't see him in the picture.

>>>>Tylergirl93 says: fuuuuck. prayers for Toby, guys

## TEXT WITH CHARLIE

gena's not answering her texts...

gena?

evie.

I'm sure it's just really hectic over there. maybe she's not near her phone

yeah maybe

we had such a bad fight

I think I'm gonna be sick

I'll come home

you don't have to

I'm coming home

## TEXT WITH EVIE

I know I said some really awful shit when we talked

you don't have to forgive me

but can you please text me?

I heard what happened and
I'm completely freaked out

Sept 28, 7:31 pm

I don't know if you have
your phone...

I guess you probably don't
know but the news says three
people died and five were
injured and they don't
know how badly or who and
that's all we know...

Sept 28, 7:43 pm

evie...

Sept 28, 7:46 pm

fuck please just text me when
you see this. I'm sorry.

## Fire Marshal's Report

**LOCATION OF INCIDENT:** 41 Bullis Rd.,
Toronto, ON M4M 2M2, Canada

**TYPE OF INCIDENT:** Accidental Fire

**CAUSE OF INCIDENT:** Overheating of color
gels and mechanical filters on malfunctioning
stage light

**FATALITIES:**

JANET LEARMEN

MARIAN LITTLE

ZACHARY MARTOCCHIO

part three

FINN

For You:

The problem with hospital gift shops is that everything costs too much, and the selection is shit. You can't get a normal journal at a reasonable price. You'll have to settle for something with an inspirational quote about God closing doors and opening windows. And, I mean, I'm not trying to be irreverent, but if God closes a door, can't you just open the door again? That's how doors work. Isn't that really a more empowering message?

Anyway, this is a stupid journal, but it's all they had, and I can't just sit here and think this stuff.

I wish I had my sketchbook. I should have hung onto that.

I should have hung onto you.

There's a beeping coming from somewhere, steady and even like a metronome driving the pace of this hospital. I'm stuffed into a plastic chair that wasn't designed for style or comfort, achy from being bottled up on a five and a half hour flight. At some point, I'm going to crash. Right now I'm wide awake.

The waiting room is packed, and it's weird because I know these people. Carl Casden is sitting about ten feet away from me, picking at the soles of his shoes. The actress who played Nicola on the show is here too. Does that mean her character's going to be returning this season? I don't know how I have it in me to give a shit. I don't, really.

It was Carl who called me, voice wrecked and wet, wanting to know who I was and was I a friend of Gena's and letting me know I could find you here, Humber River Regional Hospital, and Evie, you'd be so proud, I thanked him and acted totally normal and didn't lose my head at all about Ben fucking Evanson calling my phone, and didn't fall apart and beg to know how badly you were hurt.

Hospital means alive.

Hospital means alive.

I mean, maybe if I write it enough times.

The nurse or whatever she is at the desk in the middle of the room keeps wandering off, which is some special form of torture. Every time she stands up everyone looks up at her, which has the effect of making us look like a bunch of seagulls or something. I'm so tired that this strikes me as funny. I want to cry (nothing's funny, nothing's ever been less funny) but I'm too goddamn tired. So instead I'm scuffing my foot against the carpet in time with the beeps I hope aren't about you, aren't measuring your fucking life. (Beep, beep, beep, my Evie.)

I hope that's not coming from your room, but they haven't let me see you.

This is what I hope: that when I walk into your room you'll tell me to fuck off, that I shouldn't be here and you don't want me. I hope you scream at me. I hope you jump up from your bed and try to hit me, because I hope you jump and scream and know you don't deserve the shit I did.

Charlie hasn't returned the text I sent as I was getting in line for standby flights to Toronto. I should have sent a follow up text when I landed, but between running for a taxi and worrying about you, I just didn't do it, and now I'm in this waiting room and I have enough time to count cracked tiles and memorize the French No-Smoking signs ("defense de fumer" sounds like they're protecting the right to smoke) and browse the fucking gift shop and my phone's not getting service.

This all happened so fast, Charlie may not know I'm here yet.

He may not want me back now.

But the fucking fact of the matter is that you're my best friend and this show was the only thing you had going, and I just don't have it in me to not be here right now. If Charlie can't deal with that then I guess he doesn't love me.

And fuck it. You know? Because I love this about me.

The nurse is back now with a cup of coffee and a magazine, just flipping pages like the world's not ending. Everyone's impatient, everyone's angry, but everyone's talking in whispers because that's waiting room protocol, I guess. We're not here for this shit. We're here to see our people. Let us see our people.

Oh god, be okay, please be okay, what's taking so long.

It's so weird how we're all here for the same reason. There's a feeling of community – people touching, holding hands, hugging – going on all around me, and I can't help but resent it because I can't be a part of it. I know these people by their faces, names, voices, but they don't know me. I don't belong to them. Their fucking world exploded today, and the fact that mine did too has nothing to do with them. I want someone to bring me coffee. I want someone to rub my back and ask me how I'm doing. I'd settle for some fucking sympathetic eye contact to acknowledge that this is shared grief, that this isn't just happening to them, it's happening to me and to you and it's ours.

And fuck, I'm even allowed to be sad (fucking devastated, holy sweet jesus) about Zack.

His girlfriend's here, in the corner. Miranda. I recognize her, voyeuristically, from pictures on message boards and handed around fandom. She's alone. That seems poetic and disgusting and hilarious and I think I'm going to throw up again. They're walking in wide arcs around her, the way people do around tragedy, and she's dramatically beautiful with her makeup smeared and her model-thin body all at angles. She still looks like a model. I don't know how she can. But I don't know how I can still be sitting here wondering what Up Below is going to do without Jake, either. I guess some things are just fucking constant.

I guess I can't

Was I asleep? I think I was asleep. I swear I just looked at the clock and it was 11:45 and then now it's 12:20. There's a lot of commotion in the room now, which is probably what woke me. People are getting to their feet, not bothering to whisper, moving toward the door in clumps. The room is emptying out.

Oh. Toby's awake.

Their person. Not my person.

Everything's so surreal. I haven't slept in about a day. People have started asking me who I am. Carl Fucking Casden just came over and asked me if I was Finn, and I swear there was a second where I couldn't remember.

He had your backpack. He brought it here from the set. First me and now your backpack. He's looking out for you. It's that cute pink backpack you had in your dorm room, and I'm remembering lying on your bed, rubbing my foot against the canvas and watching you struggle through your fourth hour of homework. The bag was heavy with books then. It looks nearly empty now.

I don't want to look inside. I guess I don't want to think about what you did to get ready for the day on the morning Zack died (Jake died) (I'm a bad person).

Also, I hate that Carl is seeing me today of all days, because I always imagined I'd be charming and clever and...you know. Memorable for good reasons. Like when I met Zack at the con and he liked my art (and what difference does that make now?). If Carl remembers me, it'll be this terrible-looking mess, covered in flight and hospital and worry. You'd hate that I'm worrying, Evie; you'd tell me that worry isn't love and that you don't want me to be here because I'm afraid for you, you want me to be here because I fucking love you. And it's not until right now, in this waiting room with Carl Casden, that I understand all that worry and fear and love are all the same damn feeling.

Anyway, they're leaving and the room's emptying out and too damn quiet, and even though I was excluded from their pain, I miss them now. There's nothing to distract from the too-loud ticking of the clock, the incessant beeping, and the worry.

I wonder if they've told you I'm here.

I wonder if the delay is just that you don't want to see me (but someone would tell me, they'd have to, right?).

I'm kind of thinking of nagging the nurse about it, in the same way I'm thinking about running out of this room and out of this hospital and running and running until I can't feel any of this anymore. I'm not going to do it. I'm just going to sit here.

You'd tell me I'm being brave, but you'd be wrong.

...Oh god, Evie, Toby just screamed. <u>Toby</u>. I recognize that cry from the fucking show, from an episode in season 2. That's Tyler in agony (Toby in agony). He must just be finding out about Zack. Oh my god. Toby just found out about Zack and it's <u>killing</u> him just like it did in the show. I've heard this exact sound for this exact reason and I've loved it.

Oh god.

There's a sick, sad part of me that can't help but think how touching this would all be to the fandom. They'd be sad and sorry and they'd absolutely want to know every detail of Toby's pain. I'm not going to tell them, but I can't deny feeling a little shiver of <u>he loves Zack so much</u>.

**✖ ✖**

Evie baby baby <u>baby</u>.

It's funny (it's not funny) but the first thing I noticed when I came into your room is that you won't look at me. Before I saw the oxygen mask, before I wondered about the bandage on your

cheek, before I registered the fact that you're hugging yourself and rocking and crying, <u>really</u> crying, not trying to hide it
the way you did in the dorm. This is crying like breathing, deep
and constant and automatic and almost soothing.

But you won't look at me. I don't know if you even know I'm
here.

Look at me. Yell at me, come on, make fun of my journal. You'd
hate this journal. You'd steal it and say it's too ugly to keep to
myself and you're going to read it, and I'd let you, because it's
for you, because I'm for you.

Did you see it happen? Did you see the explosion and the fire and
whatever it was that cut your face flying toward you, and did
you understand the pain before you felt it? Did you see your
friend die? I can see in your face, through the haze of whatever sedatives they've clearly got you on, that you know what
happened. You won't be like Toby. You won't scream.

The nurse warned me that you weren't letting anyone touch
you.

But you let me hug you when I came in. My girl.

Please fucking please hear me.

I'm here now. I'm not going anywhere.

For You:

Hospitals should invest in curtains, and maybe some paint.
Something to make this place less institutional and more
comforting. If I were a doctor, I think I would set aside some
of my money for interior design of my hospital. I would make
sure my patients felt safe and at home. For you, Evie, gray

walls and a thick pink comforter and a laptop with unlimited internet access. I know what you need.

The phone reception here is so spotty that it merits wondering whether Charlie's called a dozen times (or sent me a text telling me not to bother coming home) and the signal just hasn't gone through. Anyway, there's nothing from him or from anyone.

The flowery nurse – she told me her name, but who could remember – gave you another shot late last night, which I held you still for. It wasn't really necessary. You didn't react, even when the needle went in. What I do remember is that, in a kind of shocking moment of responsibility, I asked her if whatever she was giving you was safe to take considering the meds you're already on, to which she responded that no medication had shown up in your bloodwork.

I know you didn't want to stop taking your meds. Why did you?

She tried to shoo me out. I guess visiting hours were over, but I didn't have anywhere else to go. Should have planned ahead. I was thinking we'd leave together, but I don't know what was supposed to come after that. This isn't your hometown either. Back to your hotel, I suppose. I have no idea whether or not I'm going back to Santa Rosa, and it's clear by now that you're not going back to Providence. Not like this.

So I slept in the waiting room with my head on your backpack and my feet on my journal, and consequently my hips hurt and I feel awkward and old.

I really hope you're not having nightmares. I can imagine what they'd be (of course I can't imagine it, I'll never be able to imagine what it was like). Your face is calm, but for all I know that's just another effect of the drugs. It's hard to trust anything right now.

You still haven't spoken or looked at me or acknowledged me at all.

Doctor's here...

Well, the doctor doesn't want you to leave the hospital. Apparently your "mental state is extremely fragile" and you "need full-time observation" while you're coming off the drugs they put you on. Seems like a trap to me. They gave you the drugs, and now you can't leave because of them?

I don't know what I think the alternative is. Sending you back to school is obviously a bad idea. Every time I try to call your parents I get that stupid chipper voicemail that makes me want to throw the phone at something. I know you were staying with your aunt and uncle, but none of the contacts in your phone mention those titles so I don't know if "David" is "Uncle David" or "David who let me borrow his cell phone once," or whatever. And until you start talking coherently, I don't know how I can find out. But they can't keep you here. You don't belong here, where it's too bright and no one loves you. You're not going to get better here.

And I don't like your doctor, Evie, with her condescending looks and her "Miss Bartlett, I'm not sure you appreciate the severity of this situation." I don't appreciate the severity of the situation? I don't? Who does she think took the goddamn red-eye out of San Francisco to be here? Who left her boyfriend hanging in the fucking wind? Who hasn't eaten or slept in a day and a half, Doctor?

At this point I've been with you for the past twelve hours straight and this doctor has stopped by your room one time for fifteen minutes and now she's looking at a chart and telling me she knows you better than I do.

What would you do, Evie? You'd turn on the charm. You'd tell her she's right and you understand and you agree, and before long you'd be thick as thieves and she'd be agreeing that of course you knew what you were talking about.

Me, I run away.

You know, relatively.

Specifically, to the hall.

And there goes Tyler Pierce. I guess Toby's doing better. Physically better, anyway; he looks like a ghost. He's just wandering, apparently aimless. He looked at me for a second and I feel like I'm going to drown in the awfulness.

I want to say something to him – I'm sorry about Zack – but who am I, and why should he care? I don't know Zack. I'm just a friend of a friend. I'm just some fangirl.

Maybe I need some water. Maybe I need some distance. Maybe I need to call Charlie. Maybe I shouldn't be here. I just hate everything and everybody and my heart's too big and my body's too small and I want to go home I want to go home and I don't know where home is anymore and I don't think I will ever be enough. No one's looking at me. Hospitals are a great place to fall apart in public. God, stop being crazy, Finn. No, I'm not crazy. You're crazy. No. No. No.

$$\otimes$$

Evie.

It's Charlie.

He's here. He's actually here, warm familiar hands, wrinkled clothes and messed-up hair and eyes red like the times we stayed up all night together for movie releases. He has never looked better.

I can't believe he figured it out. He's a detective, or something. I didn't tell him where I was, only that I was going. Apparently he got onto my computer (nightmare city, oh my god, if I wasn't so damn exhausted I'd be freaking out about that) and read my journal.

And he's not mad.

And I feel like everything might actually be okay.

Or at least, for the first time since I heard about the accident, I don't feel that sick sinking panic, and that's got to be a good sign.

He's talking to the doctor now, and I'm not crying so much anymore, and Toby got a Mountain Dew from the vending machine.

Somewhere your real life is going on without you. Somewhere the girls in your dorm are studying and partying and gossiping about Joanne's weird roommate who went away for a weekend and never came back. Nobody anywhere, except for right here in this too-clean too-bright hallway, is trying to figure out how you're going to live now.

We're going home, Evie.

You're coming with us. I'm taking you home.

⊗

GENA

Dr. Beatrice Monroe, MD, Humber River Regional Hospital
Patient: Genevieve Z. Goldman
October 1

For the first ten minutes of our appointment (Day 3), Genevieve was as silent as she'd been on September 29th and 30th but was beginning to show more signs of connection and interaction. She pushed herself back and forth a little in the wheelchair (despite the bandage on her hand) and picked up and played with a few of the stress toys on the table. I asked her a few questions near the beginning about how she was feeling and if there was anything she wanted to talk about, and if she understood that our session was being tape-recorded for my records. As with days 1 and 2, she didn't respond.

About ten minutes into the appointment, however, she looked up at my diploma on the wall and asked where I went to school. I told her, and asked where she went, but she was unresponsive.

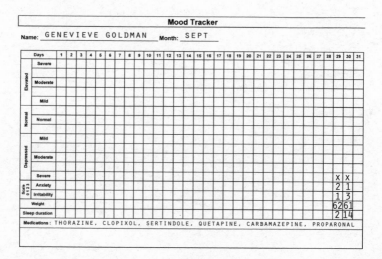

FINN

For You:

You probably look suspicious, sleepwalking around Toronto Pearson International Airport in Charlie's hoodie. It's too big for you, and you're too pale and checked out. That's probably why we had trouble at security. I should have seen it coming. I had to let go of you to send you through the metal detector, but you handled it well, at least at first. You put your hoodie and bracelets in one of those bins with your shoes, pushed it onto the belt, and walked through the gate. One of the security guards stopped you on the other side and said something I couldn't hear, and suddenly I was breathing too fast, itching to get to you. I probably looked suspicious myself.

I couldn't do anything but watch as they patted you down. It was agonizing. You've been through so much and you didn't need strange people going through your hair in a crowded place. Your fucking hair, really? What did they think, that you were carrying heroin on your scalp? Your shoulders were so tense, you were shaking and small and afraid and I couldn't get to you.

Then Charlie cleared security.

He went over, keeping a careful distance, standing in your eyeshot and smiling, and he reached into a bin and held up the hoodie. I actually saw you relax, watching him. I remember how he used to show up at my dorm the morning of exams in college and bring me omelets and joke with me so I'd be relaxed going in.

I just love him so much.

He's off getting us something to eat now, and you're calm, curled up with your head on your backpack and cuddling a juice box. You drink it quietly. I don't think anyone in the history of juice boxes has ever drunk a juice box quietly, but you do, with your knees pulled to your chest. But you're doing everything quietly now. You're still not talking much, and when you do, it's lying half the time. Stupid lies. Pointless ones. You told Charlie he didn't need to get food because you ate at the hospital, but we've both been with you all day and we know it's not true.

In the cab on the way over, you asked me why you were coming with me.

I said the first thing that came to mind. "I want you with me."

You watched me for a minute like you weren't sure if you believed me. "I should probably go to my parents. They miss me a lot when I'm off at school. They'll be upset if I go to California."

What I'm not going to say, because it's too sad and because you already fucking know, is that your parents haven't called, haven't texted, haven't been in contact with the hospital, and as far as I can tell don't read the news. Or maybe they don't get the news in Ethiopia or wherever the hell; I guess accidents on the set of third-rate cop dramas aren't exactly world headlines. Anyway, there's no indication they even know what happened. Suddenly the little annoying things my parents do – sending me recipes even though I've told them Charlie's the cook, asking about friends I haven't talked to since high school – seem endearing and familiar.

I didn't say any of that. What I said was, "please come with us. We'll go to the beach."

You nodded and closed your eyes. "I like the beach."

GROUP TEXT

hey, parents

*Oct 2, 2:41 pm*

Mom: Stephanie?

Mom: Is everything okay?

about to get on a plane

Dad: vacation?

> coming home. was in Toronto
> visiting a friend

Dad: how do you have
friends in Toronto! what else
haven't you told us!

*Oct 2, 2:46 pm*

> just wanted to say I love you
> guys.

*Oct 2, 2:48 pm*

Mom: Stephanie, honey, are
you sure everything's okay?

> boarding, g2g

It's a long flight. We've been up in the air for about four hours and Charlie's asleep against the window. You took my Jack and Coke from my tray table without asking (I would have said yes, of course, you can have anything) and drank it straight down in one gulp. Then you leaned forward, dug through the seat back pocket in front of you, and came up with a barf bag.

"Are you sick?"

"Probably. Excuse me," you called a flight attendant a few rows ahead and he came over, all smiles. "Do you have a pen? I need to fill out a form." Then that charming smile, the one I remember from Chicago. I wish I didn't know you so well, so I could believe this performance.

I don't wish that at all, obviously.

The steward gave you a pen and a flirty grin and you gave him my empty drink cup. Now you've got the bag flattened on your tray table and you're writing, head ducked so I can't see.

You could have had a page out of my journal if you needed something to write on, you know. You could have had the whole damn thing.

I've been trying to pay attention to the in-flight movie. It's a chase scene, but what's baffling is that it's been a chase scene for the past ninety minutes. A kid who looks sort of like Jesse Eisenberg but isn't is riding his bike at breakneck pace through the streets of Some City, USA, pursued by the stupidest branch of law enforcement imaginable, which even equipped with squad cars, motorcycles, and fancy weapons can't manage to stop their target.

There was an episode of Up Below like this. It was just a few months ago. Tyler and Jake were escaping on foot from a group of bad guys, I don't remember the specifics now, but I remember Jake had hurt his leg at some point and when they came to a fence he couldn't climb, Tyler turned back to fight the bad guys because he didn't want to leave Jake behind. It was a good episode. A lot of fandom didn't like it much, though. I think it was actually Tylergirl – Mallory – who posted that Jake couldn't carry his own weight in a fight, and that he was always holding Tyler back.

Jake's dead. That thought just realized itself in my head, or something, because I didn't actively think it. Zack Martocchio is dead and that's a tragedy, but Jake is dead and good God, that's what's making me cry.

We're starting our descent.

ON THE BACK OF AN AIRSICKNESS BAG
ON GENA'S TRAY TABLE

I was born with a big head, ~~too~~
I was born with a big head, too much
imagination, and no depth perception

I see no point in living but

# FEEL BETTER?
Use bag in the event of motion sickness

but to see you go on

hurry up please it's time
i am never without it

Patent US 2547097 A

For You:

Charlie put your bags in the guest room – look at that, I guess
we do need a guest room – and left to give you privacy or make
tea or line up your arsenal of psychiatric meds somewhere out of
sight, I don't know. You're sitting on the bed, facing away from
me, out the window overlooking our parking lot and the used car
dealership and, off in the far, far distance, a line of shrubbery.
This probably isn't how you pictured your first trip to California.

I offered you something to eat. You weren't interested.

I asked you if you saw it happen.

I can't believe I did that. I can't fucking believe I said that
to you.

Not that I got an answer.

I straightened up a pile of DVDs on a shelf as an excuse to move
a little closer. I'm not used to this feeling of dancing around
you. Everything came so easily in Chicago. In Providence we
fell back together without having to try. You've never been an
effort before, and it's killing me.

Charlie brought in a cup of tea and couldn't find a place to put it down, so I'm holding it. Writing's pretty hard like this, but every surface is covered. We don't have guests often. We use this space for storage, for the things we don't know what else to do with.

I am so, so, tired. I left him for you. I left you for him. I love you both. Zack is dead. Jake is dead. Everything is falling apart and I want to cry, I just want to go to pieces and not worry anymore.

It's your tea and I shouldn't, but it smells warm and homey and like someone's taking care of me, and suddenly the mug's half empty.

God, I'm going to start crying.

I just love you both so much. You're hurting so much.

God, I don't know what I'm going to do except cling to you and wait for things to start making sense.

I don't know how long we've been sitting here, but the sun's gone down and you're leaning on me, eyes half open. You haven't slept since you came off the drugs in the hospital. Sleep, Evie. Dream something nice for me.

TEXT WITH CHARLIE

you awake?

yeah. you?

...okay stupid question

*Oct 3, 3:03 am*

so...coming to bed?

*Oct 3, 3:05 am*

finn?

*Oct 3, 3:09 am*

I don't want to leave her alone, Charlie

*Oct 3, 3:12*

are you attracted to her?

*Oct 3, 3:13*

that's not the point

to me it is

really? after I left you and flew across the country in the middle of the night to be with her, twice? that's fine but whether I find her attractive is what you're worried about?

idk

well idk either

how can you not k

I've been distracted, okay?

I might be in love with two different people and that might make me the most awful person I know.

and evie's losing her mind and lying to strangers and writing weird poetry on random scraps of paper

and zack martocchio is dead, and

*Oct 3, 3:24 am*

and Jake is dead?

I'm an appalling person

come to bed, appalling person.

# >>UPBELOWFIESTA: THE PARTY NEVER DIES

October 4

Roll call:

By now, most of us have heard the news of the fire on the set of *Up Below*. A lot of really irresponsible rumors are going around, so here's my attempt to put some of those to rest – and I'm only going to post VERIFIED FACTS here, guys, no hearsay. If you've heard about any of the cast or crew, let me know in the comments, but please, no gossip, only cold hard 411.

So, the news:

We know Carl Casden is okay, because he gave an interview. In it, he mentioned a hospital in Toronto, but he didn't say who had been hospitalized.

This article suggests multiple deaths.

We have a photo of Toby Frost in an airport. You can sort of see the date on the list of flight times behind him, so we know this is after the explosion.

Anybody heard anything about Zack Martocchio, any of the writers, the showrunners, etc? Please comment!

>>>>Tylergirl93 reblogged this and added: this article confirms three deaths. Thank god Toby's okay
>>>>MioMy says: word of _EvenIf?
>>>>Tylergirl93 says: haven't heard
>>>>finnblueline says: _EvenIf is safe and with family

GENA/FINN

When Jake was my brother it was hotter,
Los Angeles and dust clouds and Spanish screaming
we drank Kool-Aid out of plastic bottles
We twisted off the caps and left them on the black floor
the one with the carefully placed fluorescent crosses
and circles
this is where you stand, this is where you move.
Zack and Genny played onscreen together
billed under their wrong names
and me and Jake undressed in the green room and drafted
text messages to Alanah

For You:

Sometimes being with you is like Chicago again, when everything
was easy and fun and falling into place. Except it's even better,
because we're together with Charlie in the room to see what we
are, and so you can get to know him, and so I can really work
out how it all fits together. He likes you. I can tell by the way
he messes up your hair when he's leaving for work, by the way
he brings home coasters from the bar because he noticed you
collecting them from around the house.

I really, really hoped it was going to fix everything.

But it's not working out that way at all, and not for any of the
reasons I would have expected. Charlie's spooked, but he's trying. I fall asleep with you as many nights as not, and it's warm
and comfortable and he looks in on us before he goes to bed

and smiles like a father, and on one memorable day he brought
a blanket and kissed your forehead and you squeezed his hand
a little as he was leaving.

Last night we all watched TV together – something frothy
with a laugh track, nothing that'd make you think too hard
about anything – and now I'm awake in the middle of the
night, staring at a blue show's-over glow on the screen and the
two of you curled up together like cats.

I wish I could say everything was better, Evie. More than
anything.

ACROSS SEVERAL OF THE COASTERS
FROM CHARLIE'S BAR


When Jake was my brother it was More than Oak
it was cottonwood swings that scraped your back
when you fell off
it was people who called me Genny
and people who called you Zack
when Jake was my brother
when things could be touched.


I know it was you because you were the one who held
me when the voices left
You were the one who pulled me away from deadlines
you were the one who cuddled me in a blanket in my
dorm on Monday nights
when you were my brother it was pornography in our
heads and we had no idea

For You:

Today was my first day back at work. At least, it should have
been. Actually, it turned out to be the day I lost my job. And
also, incidentally, the day you lost your mind.

I really didn't see this coming. I don't know how. God knows no
one could say I've been employee of the year. I guess I forgot
everyone else's sun doesn't rise and set with you. I guess I
convinced myself it was okay.

My things were in a box behind the receptionist's desk. She
handed it over without any acknowledgment that she even
knew who I was, and a manager came and escorted me from the
building, I guess in case I got violent or something. All of this
should probably upset me more than it does, but the truth is
that I'm just relieved. You've been staying home with just Charlie, who sleeps a lot during the day and just doesn't know you
like I do. He can't take care of you like I can. I want to be the
one taking care of you. Oh, hell.

There's no relief in what's happening to you, just empty horror,
and I'm sitting awake replaying it in my head instead of worrying about where the hell the money's going to come from now.

Charlie made spaghetti for dinner. He loves to cook, and I love
to eat. It's a good partnership. He was all expectant and cute
putting food in front of you for the first time, trying to hide
his anticipation in chatter about work and the extra shifts he'd
picked up because we need the money.

You pushed the spaghetti around on your plate.

"Isn't it good?" Charlie's not always so anxious to please. He
likes you. He wanted you to be happy with him. My Charlie.

You nodded, too fast, too hard.

"Evie, what's wrong?"

"Stop," you whispered, pulling your knees up to your chest. "Stop, stop..." and you were crying into your spaghetti, hands pressed to your ears, shaking your head over and over.

You're in bed now, still crying, rocking back and forth, and I've never felt helpless like this. I don't know what to do.

"Shut up," I can hear you whisper. "I'm not yours."

For You:

I woke up alone in the middle of the night. We fell asleep together in the guest bed, but when I woke up you were gone.

Charlie was in the bedroom, sprawled all the way across the mattress, no you. The kitchen was dark and empty. I checked corners. Nothing.

I've been worrying about this for days. If you ever left the apartment, you could go anywhere. This isn't your town and you're not in your right mind. You could be wandering the streets or fucking abducted or...shit, I don't want to think about it.

There are relative lulls, and then the world explodes.

No, that's not fair.

It's not fair to equate the sound of shattering glass from the bathroom with an explosion. Not now. Not anymore.

But my heart was fucking vibrating, still hasn't settled, and the bathroom door was locked and you weren't answering, and I started seeing spots, and Charlie was behind me out of nowhere shouting in his I-think-you've-had-enough-to-drink voice, his don't-fuck-with-me voice.

I've been worrying about you slipping away from me for days.

Shit, I don't want to cry, I don't want to get out of control right now.

I found you standing in the dark staring at what remains of our mirror, your hand a mess of blood and glass.

"I had to kill the real one," you whispered, in that voice I'll never forget.

POSTED ON THE FRIDGE

I know it was you because Zack was beaming in
interviews and kissing his Shakespearean love child
You were the one who was with me
You were big brother and I was little sister
We were Gena and Jake.

When Jake was my brother Zack was alive
off somewhere in someone else's fantasy
burning fiery inappropriate
your machine anatomy.

For You:

I'm on the roof tonight.

I never would have thought to come up here. This isn't something I would have done on my own.

The wind is whipping the pages in my journal, so forgive my bad handwriting. I'm having to hold the thing down with one hand and write with the other.

It's a miracle that I'm up here at all. I was coming back from checking the mail (bills, bills, and a care package from my mother that will probably include some newspaper articles about the crime rate in San Francisco and Los Angeles, because she hasn't grasped that that isn't where I live, and possibly also some Nutella). The hallway was breezier than it normally is, and on impulse I looked around the corner that leads to the fire escape exit and found it propped open.

You're lucky that alarm's been broken since we moved in.

I knew it was you, of course. I mean, practically speaking it could have been the stoners who live across the hall, or some-one looking for a quasi-romantic view of the quasi-city to make out against, but I knew.

I found you sitting on the edge of the roof and dangling your feet over, and I called out to you.

You didn't look at me. "Have you seen the stars?"

"What?"

"Come look."

I crossed the roof and sat next to you, and you didn't lean into me the way you ordinarily would. Instead, your weight shifted out, over the edge. "Do you know how far it is to the moon?"

I didn't.

"Two hundred thousand miles of empty space." You swayed in little circles, away from me, out over the empty air, back.

"Come inside, baby."

"Did I do it?"

I eased an arm around your back and pulled you close. You let me.

"See that star?"

"Yeah."

"It's mine."

"It's yours?"

"For wishing. It's my lucky star."

"Do your wishes come true?"

You were quiet so long I didn't think you were going to answer, or maybe the voices in your head were after you again, but then you leaned into my shoulder. "Sometimes."

"Sometimes is good."

"Sometimes sometimes is bad."

"I know."

You went inside then, and I'm still here because I can't come down, because I can't face going back in to my scrambled-up life and the people I'm failing. So I'm up here trying to pick a lucky star of my own.

I have no idea what I'm going to wish, though.

## WRITTEN DOWN GENA'S LEGS IN BRIGHT GREEN MAGIC MARKER

When I first met Alanah I thought she was fake
She had that blonde hair and the sexy shark teeth
Alanah's the kind of person who can wear backless shirts
Alanah makes you wonder where the tape is and where
she is tucked in

She reminded me of Nala, who was a wild-haired lizard
woman with pink eyes
she'd crawl out of anything she could decide was a tunnel
She liked to put her tongue in my ear and lick in circles,
mine
mine mine
she was the one who started fires

Alanah, Nalanah, loved me
poured herself into me like water down a drain
we never burned bright and hard and full of love
we never laughed together fought together cried and
cuddled on a dorm room bed
we never lit the world on fire

$\bigotimes$

## LEFT ON THE KITCHEN TABLE

Hey, Honey,

The school said they'd take care of getting this to you. We've
tried so many times to call your phone. We've sent you several
emails. Can you give us the number of where you're staying?

We'd love to come get you and bring you home with us. We know what happened must have been so incredibly horrifying. Come back and talk to us about it? And if you're not ready to come home, please let us know as soon as possible how to get in touch with whoever you're with and make sure they have everything they need to take care of you.

Spike and Thomas miss you...

xoxo
Aunt Jane

$\bigotimes$

OUTGOING MAIL, TORN OPEN AND TAPED SHUT

Ms. Goldman,

Oakmoor University forwarded your letter to me. My name is Stephanie Bartlett, and I'm a friend of Gena's. She's staying with me at the moment, but I passed your letter on to her so she'd know she had options.

Gena's not feeling up to talking much these days, but she's doing all right. At the moment she's in my kitchen baking a loaf of bread, which we're planning to eat tonight while we watch cartoons. Cartoons are all she wants to watch on TV right now, which I think is probably understandable.

Her recovery's going pretty well here in California – she's been attending a trauma support group and it seems to be helping – so I'm not sure uprooting her is the best idea. Please feel free to give me a call anytime at 618-555-0500. I know you must be concerned.

Sincerely,
Stephanie Bartlett

$\bigotimes$

bright lights, small room
there's a girl here about eight years old

finn put my hair in a ponytail this morning

the boy next to me smiles

I bet he could save the world
once a week

⊗

For You:

Charlie's working extra hours again, so we got stuck relying on
my dubious cooking skills for dinner. I hope you like canned
soup.

I got your Zyprexa today. I had to call your shrink in Connecticut and explain the situation. Or rather, give the barest
outline of it. "There was an accident and Gena's staying with
me for a while" seems like all the pertinent information and at
the same time none of it.

I'm not sure what I expected – maybe that she'd be sympathetic, or at least not give us a hard time – but I guess that's
not shrink protocol. I'm sure this is old news to you. You're
probably used to debating whether you should actually have
the pills she's prescribed. You're probably used to these tiny
bottles that cost $300, which I transferred from our already
miniscule savings account. I'm not sure how we're going to
afford next month's refill, or, you know, <u>food</u>. I need to get a
job, but I can't leave you here alone all day. Even though you'd

probably be fine. Probably. It's your birthday in two days and I can't even afford presents. Maybe a cake.

Jesus, not a cake, goddamn candles, fuck.

I made the soup in the microwave because I am useless at cooking, and I didn't heat yours up quite as much as I ordinarily would. You sat at the table and stirred it around and watched it spin in the bowl like it was mesmerizing, but you weren't crying into it and talking to the voices in your head so I'm calling it a win.

Trying to get you to talk about group therapy got me nowhere. You were so lively in Chicago. You talked nonstop. Now it's like pulling teeth. Apparently they didn't make you talk today, which I guess is nice of them, but I sort of wish they'd made you, to be honest. I sort of wish they'd sit you down and fucking figure out what's wrong and call me and tell me the steps to fix it and make you smile again. I know that's not how it works. I know. I do.

There's this one guy. Steven.

He was in an accident, you say. He gets it, you say. It's nice. You like him. He <u>gets it</u>.

I don't know why I'm being like this.

It's good that you made a friend. It's good that someone gets it. It's a good thing. Someone understands what you're feeling. You have someone to talk to, someone who you like.

It's just I thought that was me.

But you're okay today (you know, relatively), you're not crying, you're talking more, and I love you, and what else can I be but happy?

$$\bigotimes$$

Dear Genevieve Goldman,

It is with our deepest sympathies that we acknowledge both your recent trauma and your leave of absence from Oakmoor. Your personal belongings have been gathered and shipped to you and should arrive shortly. Please accept our dearest condolences. We hope to see you back on our campus the moment you are ready to resume your Oakmoor experience. You remain a crucial part of the Oakmoor community even in your absence.

In addition, we've begun forwarding your mail to this address, and it should begin arriving shortly.

Sincerely,

*Caitlin Fordham*

Caitlin Fordham, Dean of Students

$\otimes$

Dear Genevieve,

All of us here at Stoneyhall wanted to get in touch with you as soon as we heard about what happened, but I fought tooth and nail to get to be the one to write to you first. We are so incredibly sorry for what you had to witness, Genevieve. It's always horrible when someone in our community goes through something traumatic, and even more so when it's a bright, compassionate girl like you.

Please know that you are in our hearts and that we are always, always here for you if you need us. We hope you'll get in touch if there's any way we can help, and please contact any of us if you need someone to talk to. I've included my personal phone number at the bottom of this letter. Call anytime.

With love,
Ms. Esme Prevot
(203) 555-0533

For You:

It's late. It's dark out. Bed in a few hours.

You're on your computer.

This isn't a good idea. There is not a chance fandom isn't still blowing up (there's a choice of words, good lord, never speak out loud, Finn) over the accident. I've avoided my computer since reporting that you were alive. I don't want to see what they're saying.

The thing is that, for most of the fandom, the relevant tragedy is Jake's death. And I don't know how I feel about the fact that I'm legitimately grieving about this fictional character when real people are dead. What I do know is that Zack was your friend, and you're my friend, and you're a mess and you shouldn't have to see people crying over Jake.

I tried to stop you, or maybe just distract you, to intervene in some way. "What are you doing?"

"Checking email."

"Just email?"

You heard what I wasn't saying. "No."

"Why don't we watch a movie or something?"

"Don't want to."

"Evie..."

"Can you not, Finn? Can you just fucking not try to make everything fine for five fucking minutes?"

And that hurt, that still hurts, and I can't even deny it. Of course I'm trying to make everything fine. What would you do, Evie? You'd hug me and tell me jokes until I felt okay. But I've been doing that stuff for days, and you don't feel okay. This is too big. I can't help.

So now we've been sitting here for twenty minutes, twenty minutes of me sitting on the couch in front of you with every muscle tensed, pretending to watch some reality show but actually listening to every mouse click and every keyboard tap, and you're just now closing the computer. You look fine. You look calm. You walked around and you're sitting beside me on the couch and neither of us says a word. You stare at the TV with me, and we watch the people who aren't Jake and Tyler and don't talk about what we're doing.

I won't ask you what you saw on the computer.

You don't tell me.

You drop your cheek down to my shoulder like it's nothing.

You don't cry.

You don't cry, don't cry, don't cry.

$\otimes$

# Tylergirl93's
## JOURNAL

· · · · · · · · · · · · · · · · · · · · · · · · · · · · · · · · · · · · · · · · · · · · · · ·

### −Tyler Pierce has ruined me for life

· · · · · · · · · · · · · · · · · · · · · · · · · · · · · · · · · · · · · · · · · · · · · · ·

October 17

Okay.

I feel like enough time has passed that we can talk a little bit.

I want to open by saying what I know we're all feeling – Zack Martocchio was a good man. He gave generously of his time and talent to his fans and he's a big part of the reason why Up Below is the incorrigible show we've all come to love so much. He was lost too soon.

But the announcement that Up Below will be staying on the air is really just proof of what we all knew – that this show is adaptable and is going to remain powerful no matter what. I think this is what Zack would have wanted. I think we'll be seeing a great new evolution of Tyler – he's going to be reckless, vindictive, angry.

I'm disabling comments on this post because I don't want to get into it with a bunch of jakegirls, obviously that's not what it's about right now.

**0 Comments**

Hey Gena--

Okay so I'm sending this to four different addresses because I have no idea which one is right, because your school said you weren't there anymore and was completely unhelpful about what address to send it to or if I could just write it to them and get it forwarded because Oakmoor is some kind of shithole, babe, but hello, fake Genas. And hello real Gena too, hopefully. Either way, I hope you enjoy the swirly lollipop. I blew a lot of money on these.

I miss you, girl. Let me know if I can come out and visit, okay? We'll hit it cali-style.

Give me a call when you can, okay? Remember how we made up songs about each other's numbers to remember them?

Miss you, Gena. Nice meeting you, fake-Genas.

Love,
Alanah

$$\otimes$$

For You:

You're crying.

I can hear you in the dark, so dark I have to curl up against the window pane to see well enough to write this. It's heavy and slow, hospital crying, so quiet that I didn't realize it was happening until I felt the bed shake a little under me.

"Hey." I petted your hair. "Hey, it's okay."

You shook your head, and yeah, I know it's not. I know.

"Do you want to talk about it, Evie?"

"No." It was barely a whisper. You still haven't talked about it. It's starting to feel weird. You and I talk about everything. You're slipping away from me, and I shouldn't care so much because you're slipping away from yourself. We have to figure out how to catch you, both of us together. Please together.

"What's in your head?" I tried, pushing the hair out of your face.

"Everything. Fucking everything." You closed your eyes and lay there shaking.

I don't know what else to do, so I'm writing this with one hand on your back, singing songs from old TV shows, songs I don't know the words to, filling in the blanks with hums and random syllables. If you won't talk to me, I'll fill the space between us with whatever I have, for as long as I can.

You're still sobbing a little, quietly.

"It was my fault." You've been saying this for a while now, no matter how many times I try to rub your back and rub it out of you. "I pushed. I pushed."

I'll just stay here and breathe songs into your ear until you sleep, staring at your shaking back and out at the lights of the car dealership that stay on all night.

What if I really can't help you?

$\otimes$

GENA

Hey, Honey,

We were so sorry to hear about the accident! And I have to say, we were a little hurt that you didn't contact us. Imagine having to hear that you were involved in an explosion from a man who calls himself a key grip! We've tried so many times to call your phone. We've sent you several emails. Can you give us the number of where you're staying?

We were able to get this address from the hospital in Humber River. Please pass along my contact information to your friend Stephanie, along with this check for your incidentals while you are her guest. We understand you've taken a sabbatical from school. You're welcome in our home, if you'd prefer that, until you're ready to go back.

Spike and Thomas miss you...

xoxo
Aunt Jane

I think this is the last method I HAVEN'T tried to reach you. Can you just let me know if you're okay? I promise I won't bother you after that. I just...fuck, Gena.

-J

Victoria Falls, or Mosi-oa-Tunya is located on the Zambezi River at the border of Zambia and Zimbabwe. At its highest point it is 108 metres tall, over twice the height of America's Niagara Falls.

BUG--
THIS IS VICTORIA FALLS — THE LARGEST WATERFALL IN THE WORLD! QUITE A SIGHT. WISH YOU WERE HERE TO SEE IT! WE MISS YOU FROM ZIMBABWE!
LOVE,
DADDY

IN FINN'S SKETCHBOOK

someday I will write a perfect, epic poem
my magnum opus
and I will name it

tylergirl93 is a cunt.

I'll leave that my legacy, a huge goddamn middle finger to
anyone who thinks that
maybe this is for the best
maybe it will be a stronger show now
like anything could possibly be stronger now

like someone dying is like taking a weight off
like a little dot,
a hundred and sixty pound TV-guide-magazine boy
a hundred and thirty scrawny shivering mess in his
brother-figure's arms

a ninety pound man of the house,
now it's gone and the load is a little lighter

instead of
there is one less person to pick up this fucking shithole
of a world

we need everybody
every pair of hands and legs and fists on board to hold us
up, bracing arms across arms like cheerleaders in a pyramid
like goddamn warriors.

we need everyone
except maybe tylergirl93
because she's a cunt.

ON A CAREFULLY FOLDED SHEET
OF NOTEBOOK PAPER

Steven has fingernails that are a little too long and he crushes

Dixie cups

When they're empty.


I like your sneakers, he says, at the end of the meeting

when it's time for mingling or

for awkward phone-fiddling in the corner

texting nobody

get me out of here

I talked today
told a little story about my parents that might have been true.
Something about a birthday.

I look down at my shoes
Red, high tops, words all over them, french or english or real
I wrote them in with pen times I don't remember
john used to ask me if there were poems on them
like poems were something I could put in a place

like I have any control over where they end up
burned, on a wall in your room, washed down the drain in green
marker slime

now I conquer the world like Steven does his Dixie cup
I think today is
my birthday

ON THE BOTTOM OF FINN'S SHOES

if I hear the name jake one more time i'll scream

(if I let myself believe that tyler never will again I'll die) how do I tell steven that I lost two people

where are the funerals for dead decency
where's the hallmark card to send your parents that says
I miss him all wrong

if parents don't have to exist to be real
why should you

(i'll burn fandom to the ground)

FINN

For You:

I have to get out of the house. I can't take you walking around like the ghost of a stranger. I can't take listening to you crying in the shower and then whistling while you fix your hair like nothing's wrong. I can't deal with the way you're so on top of everything, except when you're not and I have to help you in and out of your sweaters and you slump against me and shiver and don't talk.

And I don't want to hear any more about Steven. So that's a thing.

You smiled this morning, and when I asked why, you said you were excited to tell Steven something. I can't remember the last time you smiled about me.

"He gets me," you say, the clear implication being that I don't.

And maybe it makes sense that I don't, because everything we are, whatever it is, grew out of fandom, and you are raging at fandom. You sign on to your computer for stretches of five or ten or fifteen minutes at a time, click through journals, slam it shut and sit there shaking with fury. I've tried to stop you, weirdly and passive aggressively, by piling a bunch of stuff on top of the computer and hoping you won't think about it if it's not out in the open, but that doesn't work. And maybe I should be glad you're feeling something so straightforward. But somehow, <u>angry at fandom</u> just feels like <u>angry at me</u>.

"Out of the house" in this case means Charlie's bar. I've been here for about fifteen minutes, and of course he can't come straight over. He keeps making little hand gestures that are meaningful between us – tugging his ear, biting his knuckle, this customer is an ass, I'm glad you're here.

Okay. Here he comes, with a beer I can't afford. Good thing he can tap it out for free. We need every damn dollar because your hospital bill came today. Happy belated birthday, I guess.

Even after Up Below's insurance, the copay is more than I've ever seen on a bill, ever. It's going to wipe out our savings, and I have no idea where the money's going to come from for your Zyprexa next month.

I'll have to get a job.

But the thing is that I found your shoes in the trash today, your written-on shoes, twisted so the soles cracked like maybe you didn't like what you'd written and tried to crumple them up like paper, and I'm freaking out because I left you for an hour to come down here for a beer I can't afford, so how am I supposed to leave you alone all day? How am I supposed to leave you on bad days?

Today's not a bad day. Today's a Steven day.

Steven, with his similar trauma, with his ability to relate to you, Steven who <u>understands</u>. Steven who I sent you to because I couldn't help.

And I know that's the point of the group, and I feel awful. That's the whole reason I wanted you to go, isn't it? If Steven's helping you, I want you to have him. I want you to get better.

No. I wanted you to go so you'd get better enough to talk to me. You're my best friend. I thought I was the one who understood you.

God, how selfish. I am the worst person I know.

That's a self-indulgent statement if there ever was one. I'm not <u>the worst person I know</u>. I'm jealous and insecure and I miss my best friend, and this is nothing I haven't done to you every time I prioritized Charlie. I'm not awful. I'm just sad.

Why can't Steven be there to help you out with the trauma stuff, and I'll still be your go-to person for...

For what? Fandom? You need a trauma buddy now, and you don't need me, except to pay for therapy and drugs (and apparently a new pair of shoes).

It's not gonna matter anyway if we can't figure out where to get the money to keep you in group. And despite my fucked up conflicted feelings, I do want you to stay in group.

Charlie's smiling and making drink your beer gestures, why is he fucking amazing, so what the hell. The beer is cold and light and feels like being irresponsible with everyone's heart.

So...

God.

I shouldn't have gone out.

I got home about an hour ago. You were sitting in the middle of a pile of broken laptop components, trying unsuccessfully to break a piece of casing in your hands and crying.

"Finn?"

"Yeah?"

"Did I do it?"

"Break the laptop? Yeah, baby. It's okay."

"No..."

"It's okay, Evie."

You let me sit you down on the stool in the bathroom and wash your face and hands, take down your ponytail, brush your hair, get you ready for bed. Now you're just staring at the wall and

acting like I'm not here, which I guess I might as well not be.
But I'm not going to leave you alone again tonight.

Charlie got in about ten minutes ago and stuck his head in here,
but I sent him away. Tonight it's just you and me. He kissed us
both before he left, and left behind a brown leather journal
with a cat on it.

It's much nicer than mine, and I'm jealous (for a change, ha),
but Charlie says it's for you.

Maybe we won't have to get you new shoes after all.

⊗

My favorite fics were the ones where you were cold.
I could have read those a hundred times
read each individual one
a hundred times

some of them I did, over and over
bad writing, trite clichés, the same tropes in all of them
it was the tropes that I liked.
It was you shivering that I liked.

The ones where you were cold had Tyler with a down
jacket ready to
wrap you up
they had pretty frozen fingers
scared eyes
sometimes your hair would be wet
sometimes you'd have a fever, hot really
but cold to your bones
and no one could warm you up.
But Tyler would never stop trying.
Those were my favorites.

that doesn't mean that there weren't times
that I set you on fire

I saw it
that's the thing
I saw smoke coming from that light
and I thought to myself

okayokayokay

you don't smell burning plastic mannequin skin fake LA
plastic reality machines
you don't hear anything starting to burn and whistle
you don't see smoke coming from that light
I could have pulled a fucking fire alarm

a poet
should like irony.

it matters less than what I wrote about
your shivering is bigger than my shallow breathing and
your burning alive

I scrape feelings out of your grave

making out with a tv screen

I prefer delusions
I prefer poems

with pretty line breaks

and timing

it's just that I'm waking up in the middle of the night
invisible hands on my throat, invisible smoke in my lungs
not shivering

waiting for
a part of me
to like it

IN CHARLIE'S NOTEBOOK

after group
Steven and I lie in the grass outside the rec center
waiting for finn to pull up

he taps my nose with the stem of a dandelion

What show was it again? he says

I tell him

or I tell him the name.

I don't watch much TV, he says, not like
he's judging me, not like
it matters really, just like
it's a useless fact about him
a color hair he doesn't have
something he doesn't think about
a person he doesn't know

"TV raised me," I say, and I tell him about learning sex
from Boy Meets World
drugs from Degrassi
family from Man of the House

He's never heard of any of them

a hundred voices in my head
and here is a boy who has never heard of any of me

I go home and kiss Finn's shoulders and pretend it is all
the parts of her

GENA/CHARLIE

Hi Gena. You left this in the kitchen and I thought you might want it. I'll be playing Halo if you need anything.

—Charlie

I'm here but you're not. invisHalo! --Gena

I took out the trash!!
Where the hell did YOU go, is the question.
Well. This seems like an opportunity for a treasure hunt. Let's see how quickly you find this.

gena was on the fire escape
the question is
WHERE AM I
--notebook

Notebook,
Are you sentient? You must know so many secrets. Tell me everything.

—Charlie

do my pages know secrets?
let's see if they do
if you've found where i'm hiding
you've found the next clue
--notebook

I found you in
my tv tower
after searching for
a fucking hour

but the question is
as questions be
did you note what was
underneath me?


uh. what?

for the ease
of your finding
i've slipped the clue under
a door so sliding


this picture's from the set of man of the house

it must have been the day you shot that thanksgiving scene
I remember your ugly sweater

is that why you were crying?


in fact it was!
i didn't know you watched.


Zack was my age, and it was a family show.
We always watched on holidays.
My mom used to say you were cute.

my mom said i had too-big eyes like a bug.
they still call me that.


if you're a bug you're a Tardigrade
which is a super tough bug that can survive in a vacuum
(I just Googled that.)


i used to think that
about surviving in vacuums

i used to live like that.

shrunk up and vacuum-sealed.
put me anywhere.

why do you write poems on your shoes?

in retrospect, it's dumb to think it was only because
no one had ever gotten you a notebook

so if people try to read them when i don't want them to
i can kick them in the face

god. it's a bad day.

I'll make you macaroni and cheese with bacon for dinner.
If you don't like bacon you can always pick it out, which will
be adventurous.

i do.

the truth is

we were friends when we were little because we were together
we were friends because people told us to be friends

conveniently i loved him and i think he loved me

but we didn't talk for ten years,
and we had some nice emails before he died
and i told him i was in love with your girlfriend.

the truth is
i didn't know him that well

and in the middle i had jake.

how do you NOT be a fangirl? how do you not do it?
how do you just love one person
how do you just choose everyone's real person.

you don't.

the truth is
your heart is stronger than you think it is
and bigger than you think it is

the truth is
loving someone isn't a period
it's a semicolon
and the choice you make is what comes
on the other side

maybe it's a picket fence and a subaru and 2.5 kids
maybe it's a fantasy world that lives in your computer
maybe it's a guild
maybe it's a fandom
maybe it's the last thing you ever expected

loving someone means whatever you decide it means
that's the choice
really

i love you charlie

are you gonna watch the premiere with us?

if you want me.

I'd love to.

our counselor says
you didn't get to choose what happened to you

you don't get to choose if it still hurts you

you get to choose if you put it in your sentence about
yourself.

So here is my sentence.

I love you, Zack
and fuck all the rest of it.

FINN

Dear Stephanie,

Angie and Lydia were here last weekend. We all went shopping.
I've attached a picture of them holding up their new sundresses.
We all missed you and wished you were here. Will we see you
soon?

I got a seed packet from my subscription service in the mail.
Sunflowers. I'm thinking of planting them in their own little patch
in the backyard, but sunflowers are kind of garish, aren't they? I
wonder what you think. Would that be too dramatic? Do you think
the neighbors would complain?

I haven't heard from you in a while. I hope everything's going well.

All my love,
Mom

FROM: FINN BARTLETT <FINN.A.BARTLETT@GMAIL.COM>
TO: JOAN BARTLETT <JOANBARTLETT4472@GMAIL.COM>
DATE: *NONE. SAVED TO DRAFTS.*
SUBJECT: RE: GIRLS SHOPPING DAY!

Everything's great! This picture is great! Looks like you guys had a
really good

FROM: FINN BARTLETT <FINN.A.BARTLETT@GMAIL.COM>
TO: JOAN BARTLETT <JOANBARTLETT4472@GMAIL.COM>
DATE: *NONE. SAVED TO DRAFTS.*
SUBJECT: RE: GIRLS SHOPPING DAY!

I wish I could have been there! I love Lydia's dress. Angie's looks
too orange for her. Maybe we can

FROM: FINN BARTLETT &lt;FINN.A.BARTLETT@GMAIL.COM&gt;
TO: JOAN BARTLETT &lt;JOANBARTLETT4472@GMAIL.COM&gt;
DATE: MONDAY, NOVEMBER 3 2:39 PM
SUBJECT: RE: GIRLS SHOPPING DAY!

hi mom.

glad you and ang and lyd had fun. they look great here.

no, sunflowers aren't too garish. I think they'd be pretty. and if the neighbors complain they can take a walk. it's your yard.

to tell you the truth, things aren't going so well and they haven't been for a while.

FROM: JOAN BARTLETT &lt;JOANBARTLETT4472@GMAIL.COM&gt;
TO: FINN BARTLETT &lt;FINN.A.BARTLETT@GMAIL.COM&gt;
CC: PAUL BARTLETT &lt;GOHAWKEYESFAN@HOTMAIL.COM&gt;
DATE: MONDAY, NOVEMBER 3 4:57 PM
SUBJECT: RE: GIRLS SHOPPING DAY!

What's wrong? Is it Charlie? Are you two fighting? Is it something with the job? Can I do anything to help you? You know I'm always in your corner, Stephanie. You can always depend on your parents to help you if you need it.

All our love,
Mom & Dad

FROM: FINN BARTLETT &lt;FINN.A.BARTLETT@GMAIL.COM&gt;
TO: JOAN BARTLETT &lt;JOANBARTLETT4472@GMAIL.COM&gt;
CC: PAUL BARTLETT &lt;GOHAWKEYESFAN@HOTMAIL.COM&gt;
DATE: MONDAY, NOVEMBER 3 3:16 PM
SUBJECT: ISSUES

thanks you guys.

things with Charlie are okay. we had kind of a bad patch, but I think we've worked it out. it was rough for a while. but it's Charlie.

to tell you the truth, and please, please don't start calling everyone and telling them this, especially not angie and lyd because you know they'll be all over my case about it, but I think we actually might get married.

not that he's asked. not that I've said yes. but I feel sort of like if he did, I would. I just feel like he knows me as well as any one person can and still loves me, and after almost four years I still love him, and...you know? I've never done this before. is that how it's supposed to feel?

anyway, that's future stuff. for the time being I'm happy with the way we are.

the job...well, I lost the job. I'm sorry I didn't tell you sooner. I'm sorry I can't figure out how to be gainfully employed. I'm sorry I'm letting you down. I'm broke and embarrassed and it feels awful, and as much as I want to stay here and live this life, I might not be able to afford it much longer.

the truth is, my best friend was in a bad accident, and now she's got some kind of post traumatic stress thing and no money to pay for the drugs she needs. she's living on our couch and I've been paying for group therapy because I can't afford the one on one kind, and my savings account is dry and her aunt has been sending money for her meds, but I don't think Evie ever told her how much they cost and I don't feel comfortable asking this woman for money, and anyway I can't use that to pay the bills, obviously.

So things are pretty messed up right now.

FROM: JOAN BARTLETT <JOANBARTLETT4472@GMAIL.COM>
TO: FINN BARTLETT <FINN.A.BARTLETT@GMAIL.COM>
CC: PAUL BARTLETT <GOHAWKEYESFAN@HOTMAIL.COM>
DATE: MONDAY, NOVEMBER 3 5:44 PM

Oh, Sweetheart.

You should have told us you were in trouble. Of course we're not disappointed.

You stay strong, like you always do. We are so proud of you, Stephanie. Helping a friend in trouble – that's exactly the kind of girl you've always been, ever since you were young. Is this friend someone we know? She's lucky to have you in her life.

We have some extra money that was earmarked for you, since you won a scholarship and your sisters didn't. Would that give you some breathing room until you're able to find a new job?

Love,
Mom & Dad

FROM: FINN BARTLETT <FINN.A.BARTLETT@GMAIL.COM>
TO: JOAN BARTLETT <JOANBARTLETT4472@GMAIL.COM>
CC: PAUL BARTLETT <GOHAWKEYESFAN@HOTMAIL.COM>
DATE: *NONE. SAVED TO DRAFTS.*
SUBJECT: RE: ISSUES

no, I can't

FROM: FINN BARTLETT <FINN.A.BARTLETT@GMAIL.COM>
TO: JOAN BARTLETT <JOANBARTLETT4472@GMAIL.COM>
CC: PAUL BARTLETT <GOHAWKEYESFAN@HOTMAIL.COM>
DATE: MONDAY, NOVEMBER 3 4:01 PM
SUBJECT: THANK YOU

I don't know what to say.
Thank you so much.
Thank you for believing in me.
I love you both.

GENA

## What Steven Said

our group leader says
trying to break out of it is no way to live

he says
stretch inside of it
there is so much room
there is so much for you to grab in here
stop hurting yourself trying to escape
just
stretch

steven thinks he means mental illness
I think he means our past
I think he means our family

we're lying on the grass again, me and him
while he tickles the bottom of my foot with a blade of
grass
because I don't have shoes on

I tell him that I feel like i'm lying to him
and he looks up

"Why?"

"Because I haven't told you everything," says me.

He crawls up me, elbows on either side of my ribs, all
breathing and skin and friend

"I haven't told you everything either," he says.

and I realize

I don't want to tell him.

not because I don't want him to know
not because I want to be able to run away
not because I think he couldn't take it

because i'm tired
because it would take such a long time
because maybe I am beginning to forget parts
and maybe that's okay

because I am lying in the grass with a nice boy
who doesn't need to be everything

I stretch out

Text with John C.

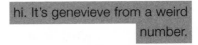

*Nov 5, 5:16 PM*

honey.

What Finn Said

the premiere's in three days
we're eating popcorn
to practice

"do you ever want kids?" I say

she tosses a piece in the air
catches it in between her teeth
like an expert

this girl could do anything.

"nah," she says.

"i have a kid," she says.

She puts her hand on top of my head, tugs me in.

"you're the best kid in the world
and we made you that way ourselves."

$\otimes$

What Gena Says

i thought that the fire would always divide
this is now, that was then
i thought it was a line break
like a new stanza
you can't go back.

i thought grief would insert itself in the middle and never leave.

i know better now.
stanzas are for quitters
punctuation is for the brave.
If love is a semicolon then grief is a comma:
it won't ever stand alone,
but it will give you one breath,

in.

$\bigotimes$

FINN

For You:

You're probably wondering why I'm telling you all this.

You were there for almost all of it. There's not much I can say that you don't already know.

The Season 4 premiere aired on a Monday. I wish it didn't. I wish they'd moved it to Wednesday, or Friday, or nine a.m. on Sunday morning. Monday night was when we watched Jake. This is a different show, and any loyalty I feel (and there is some, I can't deny it) is residual and unearned. Tyler's fine, but who is he now?

On the night of the premiere, you and Charlie were giddy and ridiculous, and it surprised me to see either of you so worked up about the show. "What's going on?"

"Surprise present!" you said, and Charlie shot you a look like you wrecked Christmas.

"The hell? It's not my birthday."

"It's not really a present, either." Charlie handed me a newspaper-wrapped bundle. "It's already yours."

"It's my sketchbook!" I could tell immediately by the size and weight. "Where did you get it?"

"I had it, remember?" You were nearly bouncing up and down. "You left it in my dorm. You told me to keep it. Like I was going to."

"Don't worry," Charlie grinned. "I didn't look at it."

"I looked at it," you informed him.

"Fangirl stuff," he said knowledgeably, and not like it was a bad thing either. Like it was ours, mine and yours.

So I've got that back now, and it's such a relief, and you're probably wondering why I'm still writing everything down in this stupid expensive uninspiring gift-shop journal.

We had dinner (lasagna, Charlie cooked) at the table like it was an occasion and filed into the living room ceremoniously when we'd finished. Charlie settled in his La-Z-Boy with his computer on his lap, which is the way he's always watched Up Below. He doesn't have to pay attention, really. It isn't his show. He watches for the chase scenes and the fights, and occasionally the plot. He likes Evanson.

You wore his hoodie and my yoga pants because your clothes still haven't arrived from Oakmoor. (I don't know who was in charge of boxing up your things and shipping them to us, but they should be fired.) You had a chocolate bar, which you weren't eating. I don't really blame you. I was too nervous to touch my dinner.

I want to say I feel like the premiere shouldn't have been such a big deal, but the truth is that I can't imagine why it wouldn't be.

I saw it coming before it happened. We all did. Tyler walked out of a crumbling cave without checking to see if Jake was behind him, which was so out of character that I actually giggled. I clapped a hand over my mouth and looked at you, at Charlie, but he was rolling his eyes and your mouth was quirked a little in a way that let me know you weren't upset.

There was a recycled shot of Jake looking up – any fan would have spotted it, even Charlie knew – a rumble of falling rock, a moment of silence, and that's it.

The worst part was when Tyler screamed.

That was recycled too. I recognized it from Season 1. They didn't ask Toby to do that, and I'm glad.

The rest of the episode was mostly Evanson, which means it was pretty boring unless you actually care about things like plot and politics. By the half hour mark, I had my sketchbook out, working on something that's probably going to be Jake when I get it done. I can't help it. I miss him. Charlie was actively ignoring the TV, and you were making short work of the chocolate.

"Do you guys want to turn it off?" I looked around for the remote.

"Nah," you said through a mouthful. "Might as well see how it ends."

How it ends, predictably, is with Tyler (who I keep thinking of as Toby now) vowing to avenge Jake's death. It was nice of him, I guess. We all know it can never make anything right. Evanson revealed himself to be one of the good guys, probably (tune in next week!) and the end credits included a title screen in memoriam of Janet Learmen, Marian Little, and Zack Martocchio.

I don't feel anything about any of that.

You're probably wondering why I'm telling you this, because you saw that episode, and I don't think you felt anything either. When it ended you looked at me and shrugged and said "There that is, then," and went to take a shower. Just now I went to check on you and you were already asleep in bed, curled around Charlie's laptop with your journal pulled up. You've been writing something. I left it there, in case you want to finish when you wake up.

I'm telling you this, Evie, because stories change in memory and in the retelling, and because you write and rewrite them until they're what you want them to be, but this is one story

I want you to remember the way it happened. I want you to remember the people we are now, the times I was there for you and the times I let you down. I want you to love me weak like I loved you crazy, and when we're both on top again we'll remember that we did it.

$\otimes$

GENA

**_EvenIf's** **Journal** / I watch a lot of *Up Below* and write a lot of fanfic and shoot a lot of heroin. One of those is false. I do a mean French braid.

## (NOV 7) Here goes.

**Title:** Here. You. Me.

**Author:** _EvenIf

**Word Count:** 262

**Summary:** Post-4x01

**Pairing:** none

**Disclaimer:** don't own the characters

**Author's Note:** I wrote this whole long intro and deleted it, so...here's what I have to say. Hope you like it.

If you'd asked Tyler what he would miss most if he ever lost Jake, he would have known the right things to say. His laugh. The shit he leaves all over Ty's damn car. The awful singing. Push him a little harder and he would have begrudgingly mentioned some sentimental stuff: floppy cakes Jake attempted on his birthdays, the smell his shampoo left in the shower. And that fucking laugh, again.

He's never going to forget the laugh, but what he never thought would hit him so hard is how much he's hurting for how fucking loud Jake was when he was sleeping.

Because Evanson's gone now, and it's just the dark and this scratchy unfamiliar mattress and *nothing else*, and fine, FINE, if it's his responsibility to fill the silence he'll fucking cry, okay?

It's familiarity, it's childhood, it's security, it's a brother.

And it's the end of Jake so it's the end of part of him and what he wants to know, what he just wants to know right this fucking minute is *how much of him*, because if you'd asked him before, if you'd asked him how would you be if Jake died he would have said I WOULD DIE, THERE WOULD BE NOTHING THE HELL LEFT OF ME--

but here he is.

And he just wants it to be tomorrow so he can sit up and look at himself in the light and see what's left of him.

"I can't keep going," he says, tamping down the quiet, just for a minute.

He breathes, accidentally, and keeps going.

--genny goldman

and since I promised you all some pictures:

Me filming a scene with Jake, two days before the accident:

⊂⊐ <up_below251.jpg>

Me and Zack on Man of the House during a break, drinking juice boxes (we had to practice drinking them SILENTLY so we could have them while other people were filming):

⊂⊐ <juiceday.jpg>

and a gorgeous, GORGEOUS piece of fan art from last night, by my best friend in the world:

## 15 Comments

Leave a comment

**DanniRice**

goddddd gorgeous. Needed this, thank you. I hope we get to see something like this next week...Ty's got to have some breakdown, right?

**SwingLowMySweet**

Honey. How are you?

> **_EvenIf**
>
> doing okay. I'm sorry I left you guys hanging for so long.
>
> > **SwingLowMySweet**
> >
> > shh, no. Let me know if you need to talk, okay? Love you.
> >
> > > **_EvenIf**
> > >
> > > Love you.

**Tumbledown**

God, sobbing. I'm so glad you're okay.

> **_EvenIf**
>
> me too.

**MioMy**

holy shit.

**slotohes**

we've been SO worried about you, gena!! SO good to hear from you.

> **_EvenIf**
>
> good to be back, thank you.

**finnblueline**

you.

> **_EvenIf**
>
> you.

**Tylergirl93**

really pretty, but shouldn't you be writing about zack, not jake?

**_EvenIf**
lol

**finnblueline**
lol